W9-CEI-394

WAKE UP
MISSING

ALSO BY KATE MESSNER

The Brilliant Fall of Gianna Z.
Sugar and Ice
Eye of the Storm

WAKE UP
MISSING

KATE MESSNER

WALKER BOOKS FOR YOUNG READERS
AN IMPRINT OF BLOOMSBURY
NEW YORK   LONDON   NEW DELHI   SYDNEY

First published in the United States of America in September 2013
by Walker Books for Young Readers, an imprint of Bloomsbury Publishing, Inc.
www.bloomsbury.com

For information about permission to reproduce selections from this book, write to
Permissions, Walker BFYR, 1385 Broadway, New York, New York 10018
Bloomsbury books may be purchased for business or promotional use. For information on bulk
purchases please contact Macmillan Corporate and Premium Sales Department at
specialmarkets@macmillan.com

Library of Congress Cataloging-in-Publication Data
Messner, Kate.
Wake up missing / by Kate Messner.
pages   cm
ISBN 978-0-8027-2314-7 (hardcover) • ISBN 978-0-8027-3547-8 (e-book)
[1. Science fiction. 2. Adventure and adventurers—Fiction. 3. Genetic engineering—Fiction.
4. Friendship—Fiction. 5. Everglades (Fla.)—Fiction.] I. Title.
PZ7.M5615Wak 2013   [Fic]—dc23   2013012021

Book design by Nicole Gastonguay
Typeset by Westchester Book Composition
Printed and bound in the U.S.A. by Thomson-Shore Inc., Dexter, Michigan
2 4 6 8 10 9 7 5 3 1

For my big brothers, Steve and Tom.
I forgive you for beating up my stuffed animals

WAKE UP
MISSING

1

IF YOU HIT YOUR HEAD hard enough, your brain gets shaken up inside your skull. You might see stars or pass out for a few minutes, and after that, a bunch of things happen. It doesn't matter how you got hurt—whether you slipped on ice or had a car accident or fell from a tree. People will start flashing lights in your eyes, talking about concussions and traumatic brain injury. And even though your head hurts and you're exhausted, they won't want you to go to sleep.

They'll shake you awake every couple hours, shining lights, asking questions. Your head will throb, and you'll be dizzy, and you might throw up.

But that's not the worst part.

The most terrifying thing about hitting your head so hard is when you wake up missing pieces of yourself. Pieces of the person you were before it happened.

Things you should remember—who found you after you fell from the tree stand, why you were dizzy and hadn't eaten lunch, what kind of bird you were trying to see when you leaned forward too far—are gone. Things you could once do—kick a soccer ball without losing your balance, play air guitar with your best friend, climb into a kayak, or stand steady on the houseboat deck to pinch dead blossoms off the geraniums—all gone. Erased. Whole pieces of you are missing because your brain bumped against your skull.

That's why I wanted to go to I-CAN. As soon as Mom showed me that *Scientific American* article about the International Center for Advanced Neurology, I could tell she thought it was the answer. The feature talked about I-CAN's revolutionary treatment program combining traditional drugs with light and oxygen treatments, exercise, and gene therapy. "MIRACLE CLINIC IN THE SWAMP," the headline called it, and a miracle was what I needed.

I believed it, too. I thought if I went to I-CAN, I'd wake up found.

And all the missing parts of me—lost balance, scattered memories—would snap back into place like the jigsaw-puzzle pieces Mom pulled out from under the wicker sofa. She blew the dust off and placed them into the holes in our carnival scene, one by one, until the last piece patched an empty gap in the sky. And then it was whole.

That was what I wanted. To be whole again.

There are plenty of hospitals around the country with head-injury clinics, but at first, Mom and Dad hated the idea of sending me away. Before I was born, they thought they'd never be able to have kids. Then I showed up, an only child, wrapped up in love. I'd never even been to camp, and that was fine with me.

When we read about I-CAN, though, everything changed. I watched Mom's and Dad's frustrated faces fill with hope and possibilities. Maybe if I went, I'd be normal again. Maybe I'd be happy again. Those maybes found their way into my heart, too. I told Mom and Dad I wanted to go.

Then everything came together so quickly—the referral from my pediatrician, phone calls, work schedules rearranged, plane tickets booked, plans whipped up as fast as instant brownie mix.

I didn't have time to get nervous. Not until Mom and I stopped for lunch at Camilla's Grille in Everglades City, right before I got admitted.

The air was thick and wet, full of mosquitoes and deerflies, and all around my feet, little black crabs scuttled up through cracks in the deck, playing hide-and-seek in the shadows.

The waitress almost stepped on one when she came out of the main dining room. Kelly, her name tag said, looked about Mom's age and wore a faded, rumpled apron tied over a T-shirt and cutoff jeans.

"Your order's about done," she said, and propped open the swinging screen door with a big conch shell. A crab got trapped in the little triangle it made with the wall of the building. It kept running along the edges, looking for a way out.

Thunder rumbled, and wind fluttered our shade umbrella. "I hope this storm isn't bad," Mom said. She slid the bucket of paper towels and ketchup to the side, reached across the table for my hand, and smiled a tight smile. "Remind me again. No more than eight weeks, right?"

"Look on the bright side," I said. "Eight weeks without loud music or soggy water shoes left on the kitchen floor. Fifty-six whole days before you find another sticky, peanut-butter-covered spoon in the sink." Mom jokes that my favorite snack is the bane of her existence, so I thought that would make her laugh. Instead, her eyes welled up.

She blinked and spun the paper-towel roll around in its bucket. "I know this is where you need to be to get better." Mom missed the old Cat, I knew. She wanted her daughter back, the one without the mood swings and headaches. The one who could have fun and be happy.

I wanted that, too. But it was still awful saying good-bye to Dad at the airport. Good-bye to the cool wind off the bay and our houseboat that rocked me to sleep at night. Good-bye to my bedroom with its faded denim bedspread. Good-bye to the big oak tree silhouette that Aunt Beth painted, branching all over one butter-yellow wall with little shelves that held my clay birds. I only brought one with me here—the cardinal—because it reminded me of Mom's reddish hair.

I looked up at her. The humidity here made her curls all frizzy and wild. I smiled. "You look kind of like Lucy's poodle right now."

She laughed and then took my hand across the table. "I'm going to miss you so much."

"It'll go by fast." I looked down at a grease-stained newspaper someone left on our table. My welling-up tears blurred the headlines, but I could still read them.

· TERROR SUSPECT NABBED IN LONDON ·
· FLORIDA SENATOR PROMISES CRACKDOWN ON NATIONS THAT

HARBOR TERRORISTS: WILEY SAYS MILITARY INTELLIGENCE
COMMITTEE HAS "SECRET WEAPON" ·
· CITY COUNCILOR CALLS FOR ADDED WATER USE RESTRICTIONS ·
· NEW NATURE CENTER OPENS DOORS TO VISITORS ·
· POACHERS ELUDE FISH AND WILDLIFE AGENTS ·
· DRY SEASON BRINGS RECORD WILDFIRES:
WEATHER SERVICE SAYS FORECAST OFFERS LITTLE RELIEF ·

"Cat? You okay?"

"Of course." I blinked fast and turned my attention to the four old guys eating oyster sandwiches at the table next to ours; one still had a price tag on his fishing hat. Beyond them, a young couple was smooching at a table way in the corner.

"Are you sure you want to do this? Because—"

"I'm sure." I wasn't, but I told Mom what she needed to hear and turned away from her, toward a tired-looking guy sitting by himself at the bar, next to the speakers. Mud streaked his pants and shirt and even the notebook next to his beer. The music was so loud the waitress had to shout over "Cheeseburger in Paradise" when she said "Hey, Brady!" and asked if he wanted the usual. He shouted yes; I could hear him all the way out on the deck. She asked what he was working on, and he shook his head and flipped some pages in the notebook, but I couldn't hear what else he said.

Then the waitress hurried back to the kitchen and picked up our plates—crab cakes and salad for Mom and a cheese quesadilla for me. I wasn't hungry, but ordering was better than admitting my stomach hurt as much as my head.

The waitress pushed the newspaper aside to make room for my plate and frowned. "Haven't seen this kind of trouble with poachers in years," she said. "Got a few fellows who come in here late, all covered in mud, with flashlights in their belts, and I wonder. Makes me worry about letting my boys go out in the canoe, but they sure do love to fish."

Mom glanced at the waitress's name tag and smiled. "How old are your boys, Kelly?"

"Fourteen, twelve, and eight." She pointed out the back window of the restaurant, where a short kid was practically tackling two taller ones as they played basketball. Kelly smiled and shook her head a little. "They're a handful. You need anything else?"

"No, this looks great." But Mom frowned when the waitress walked away. "I don't like these poacher stories." She sighed. "But the clinic building is a former military base. I'm sure it's safe, and I know this is your best chance for a full recovery."

Full recovery. My head pounded under the words. It had only been a few months since my fall, but I couldn't remember a day without headaches, without losing my balance and my train of thought. I wondered if I'd recognize my old self.

Mom picked at her salad, and I moved tortilla triangles around on my plate until the waitress brought our check.

Mom took a deep breath and smiled. I could tell she was trying not to cry. "Ready to go?" she asked, tossing a twenty on the table and reaching for her backpack. "The airboat will be waiting."

"Yep." I stood up. That dumb crab was still trapped behind the propped-open door, running along the wall, back and forth, over and over. "One second." I moved the screen door, reached down, and cupped my hands around the tiny crab. It didn't pinch me, but its little legs prickled my palms. It was still frantic, looking for a way to escape. The second I put it down, it scuttled away and disappeared down a crack.

It made me wish I could go home, too. Back to San Francisco with Mom. Dad could pick us up at the airport, and we could all go to the houseboat and eat spaghetti and watch pelicans diving for fish out the window.

No, I reminded myself. *Mom and Dad want you here, to get better. And you want to be here, too.*

I ignored the awful knot growing in my stomach and followed Mom down to the dock.

2

"WATCH YOUR STEP; WE DON'T want any more bumps on your head."

Sawgrass Molly—that's what she said to call her—stood on the dock in muddy boots, work pants, and a long-sleeved shirt, with a red bandanna tied around her neck. A long gray braid hung down her back, and the skin on her face looked tough as a sea lion's.

Mom introduced herself and me, and Molly loaded our bags onto the airboat.

"Come on aboard, Miss Cat." Molly reached down to help me onto the deck, but a wave of dizziness washed over me.

I closed my eyes and tried to catch my balance, but suddenly, I was there in the tree stand again, my stomach in knots over what had happened in the school cafeteria that day, and watching—was it a northern spotted owl? Closer . . . leaning . . . leaning . . . tipping . . . flailing back toward the platform too late . . . and falling . . . falling . . .

"Cat?" Mom said my name softly. She had to do that a lot, to bring me back.

"I promise you this boat is swamp-worthy," Molly said, her brown, spotted hand still stretched out toward me. When I held it and stepped down, the boat dipped and bumped against the dock. I held on tighter.

"You okay?"

"I'm fine," I lied. Would I ever be fine again? "Guess I need to get my sea legs."

I slid into a seat and rummaged through my bag for my bird book while Molly looked past me, waving to a freckly teenaged boy and a short, tired-looking woman walking beside him.

The kid was Ben, with his aunt Wendy, from Washington State, I learned when Mom started chatting. I moved to a seat away from the boat's giant fan and controls, away from the conversations, and opened my bird book. I could tell Mom wanted me to come over and talk, make friends, but I couldn't. My head hurt, and I was afraid I'd say something grouchy or mean and make Mom cry, and she didn't need that right now.

White-and-black birds on the page blurred to gray, and I had to close my eyes. I didn't want friends here. I wanted Lucy.

We'd been best friends since third grade, but she'd sort of faded away when we started middle school, and especially since my concussion. Too much was different. I never knew when my headaches would come, so I was always on edge, waiting, wondering if I'd be this way forever.

I had to give up soccer a month into the season. I was never good at it anyway. I'd only signed up because Lucy was so excited.

The first day of school, she was my partner for drills, but I kept messing up. I couldn't help watching the girls' cross-country team, laughing together and running into the hills where the trails snaked all through the trees, while we kicked balls back and forth on the same green rectangle. The second day, Lucy was already doing a drill with Mae Kim when I got to practice, and they were partners every day after that. But I still sat near them on the bus, and I cheered for Lucy from the bench until I quit.

Now she never called anymore, and I missed so much school I hardly ever saw her in class. I used to be one of those kids who never got sick, but these last few months had been different. I'd wake up feeling okay and go to class, but by sixth period, my head hurt so bad I felt like throwing up. I did once, all over my math quiz because Mrs. Stillman didn't want me to leave until I finished.

I missed who I used to be, and if this clinic in the middle of nowhere could bring me back, it was worth anything. I forced my eyes open and turned around. Everyone was looking at me.

I tried to smile. "Hi. Sorry, I'm woozy from the boat."

They all nodded, but only Ben looked as if he really understood. His eyes stayed on me for a second before he turned back toward the water. His aunt started to say something, but Molly started up the airboat and drowned her out. That thing was *loud*.

Molly handed out earplugs, then looped the airboat in a circle to turn around. I hadn't slept well the night before, and my head was still throbbing, so I put in the earplugs, lowered my head to my hands, and closed my eyes.

I don't know how far we'd gone—maybe half an hour—when the boat slowed and Molly called out over the idling engine.

"Alligator!" She pointed. "See it? Small one, up on the bank." It was all stretched out, sunning itself, still as stone. "Soon, we'll come up on One-Eyed Lou. She has babies in the nest, though, so we can't get too close."

The airboat's fan roared back to life, and we cut through the swamp, pushing through tall grasses that blew in waves. When we rounded a bend in the river's path, Molly slowed the airboat and shouted, "Don't lean, but if you look off to the side there . . . see the trap in the water?" I made out the murky lines of some kind of cage.

"What's that?" Ben asked.

"Blue crab trap." Molly grinned. "Better known as dinner. I got a few out here, check 'em around sunset. They're great eating."

She maneuvered the airboat around another snaking curve, then killed the engine. "Keep your eyes open, because up here on the left . . ." She craned her neck. "Yep, see? That's One-Eyed Lou."

"Whoa!" Ben stood up until Molly's glare set him back in his seat. "He's huge!"

"She. Lou's a she. She's about eight or nine feet, but there are plenty bigger," Molly said. "You won't find a more aggressive gator, though. You get near those babies, and she'll snap at you like nobody's business. Take you right off your feet with that tail."

She kept the engine off and paddled the airboat ahead, where the shoreline was cluttered with a mess of tree trunks and roots all tangled on themselves. "These are mangroves," she said. "They make islands all over the swamp. Most of the small ones are quiet, a few old plume hunter's camps—I been known to spend a night or two in those when weather comes in fast."

"You sleep out on some island by yourself?" Ben raised his eyebrows. "Don't people think that's weird?"

His aunt elbowed him, but Molly laughed. "Doesn't much matter what they think. You can't let other people decide who you're going to be."

She peered into the tangled branches. "Look close in here. You'll see a couple poachers' huts." Weathered wooden boards showed through the trees.

"There was something about poachers in the newspaper." Mom's voice wobbled, but Molly didn't seem worried.

"Yep. They go after alligators. Plume birds. Sometimes endangered butterflies. But you stay outta their way and you're okay." The airboat drifted toward the trees, and we had to duck to keep our heads out of the branches.

Molly started the engine again and brought us through a wide tunnel of mangroves. "Here we are. . . ." She hit the throttle as we pushed out of the trees, onto an open lake. A huge island stretched in front of us. There was a dock, a modern-looking building that looked half hotel and half hospital, and an older building that might have been a garage or airplane hangar.

The airboat drifted up to the dock, where a man with curly brown hair waited in shorts and a faded blue golf shirt. Two kids who looked about my age stood behind him—a boy with dark skin and wire-rimmed glasses and a short, skinny girl with a bouncy, dark-brown ponytail. She plopped down on the dock and plunked her feet into the murky water, while the curly-haired guy waved us in. "Welcome, welcome, everyone. Good trip, Molly?"

"Just fine." She looked like she was about to say something else, when an osprey swooped down from a dead tree and dove straight into the water.

The girl jumped up, water dripping down her pale ankles. "That bird's got a fish!"

In its talons, the bird clutched a fish nearly as large as itself. But the fish was fighting back. Its tail slapped the water as the osprey tried to take off with it.

"What kind of fish is that?" Ben asked.

"Looks like a snook," Molly said, squinting. The sun flashed on the splashing water as the fight continued. "Maybe a bigger one than that bird can handle."

I'd seen birds catch fish before on the docks at home, but never a fish that size. Molly was right; it was *too* big. No matter how many times the osprey tried, how hard it pumped its wings, it couldn't fly. In fact, the bird looked exhausted, and the fish was starting to pull it down into the water. "Why doesn't the bird let go?"

"Can't," Molly said. "Has its talons in too deep."

I could feel the osprey's panic as it struggled. We watched as bird and fish battled in the glittering water, until finally, the osprey went under for the last time and disappeared.

"Whoa," Ben whispered.

"It truly couldn't let go, and the fish overpowered it." Molly shrugged, as if this sort of thing happened all the time here, not just on TV nature shows. "Sometimes the prey wins."

Finally, we turned our attention back to the man on the dock as he tied the airboat to a post.

Dr. Mark Ames. Back then, I thought he looked a little like my uncle Steve, with dimples and a young face, younger than the rest of him.

"Welcome to the clinic, Ben . . . Cat. I want you to meet Quentin and Sarah." He gestured toward the two kids who'd been waiting with him. "They arrived two weeks ago, and they're already feeling quite a bit better, so they'll help me out giving you and your parents the grand tour. You can leave your suitcases and backpacks right here on the dock; our orderlies will take them to your rooms. Should we start with the pool?"

"The pool . . . where you're not allowed to dive, splash, or otherwise overexert yourself," Sarah said, rolling her eyes.

Quentin grinned. "She's still mad they made her get off Trent's shoulders in the shallow end last week."

"Do you like to swim?" Sarah asked. "Or play Frisbee or shoot baskets?"

"Umm . . ." I couldn't imagine doing any of those things the way my head was throbbing. But she looked so excited. "Maybe when I feel better."

Mom gave me a tentative smile. I knew what she was thinking. *It's nice here. They have a pool . . . and birds. Remind me that this is the right thing, that you'll be happy and safe, so I can leave you without falling apart.*

I smiled back at her and reminded myself this was where I

needed to be to get better. I liked the birds. The kids were friendly, and Dr. Ames seemed nice, too. Like he cared about us, like he wanted to make sure we felt safe and happy. Like we were important to him.

I guess we were, in a way. Just not the way we thought.

3

"WOW," MOM SAID AS WE walked up the sidewalk to the swimming-pool area. "Are you sure you don't need parents to stay and chaperone? Or do dishes or anything? I could get used to this."

It was beautiful—a sparkling Olympic-size swimming pool with cushioned deck chairs and tables with shade umbrellas mixed in. There was a paved area with a basketball hoop and a net for badminton or volleyball over on the lawn.

"Even if you're not up for much physical activity yet, you can bring your lunch out," Dr. Ames said. He frowned and pulled a cell phone from his pocket. "Excuse me one moment."

"Watch out for seagulls, though," Sarah said, kicking off one of her flip-flops and skimming her toes along the water. "One swiped half my turkey wrap yesterday."

But there were no seagulls around then. And there were no other people. "Where is everybody?" I asked.

"Everybody like who?" Sarah kicked some water at Quentin.

"We're here. You're here. Kaylee never does anything fun, so I bet she's in her room."

"Probably sleeping. Dr. Ames told us her injury was more severe, so we never see her," Quentin explained. "She just goes to treatment and sleeps a lot. And Trent—"

"—is a big jerk," Sarah interrupted. "He was supposed to shoot hoops with me after dinner last night but he never came outside. I haven't seen him today, either." She turned to Dr. Ames, who was tucking his phone back into his pocket. "Hey, Trent didn't leave or something, did he?"

Dr. Ames chuckled. "Relax, Sarah. Trent's doing great, but I'm sure he would *never* go home without saying good-bye to his basketball buddy." He turned to Mom and me. "Trent is in the final stages of Phase Three, so he's spending more time in treatment these days. But Cat will meet him soon, I'm sure."

"Now Phase Three is . . . the gene therapy?" Mom asked, even though she'd read everything on the I-CAN website a zillion times.

"Exactly," Dr. Ames answered her, and turned to me and Ben. "Do you guys understand how that works?"

"Kind of," I said.

Ben shrugged like he didn't care how it worked, but Dr. Ames included him in the conversation.

"Well, when you guys got your concussions, it damaged your brain tissue. That's why your heads hurt so often, why your vision gets blurry, and you can't always seem to think and remember stuff the way you used to. In order to fix that for you permanently, we need to replace the damaged tissue with healthy brain cells."

"You happen to have some healthy ones sitting around?" Ben sounded skeptical.

His aunt nudged him. "Don't be rude," she whispered, but Dr. Ames chuckled.

"They're not *that* easy to come by, Ben." Dr. Ames smiled at him. "I appreciate a man who's not afraid to question things. But I do like to think we work some magic here. We have a process that can actually *make* healthy brain cells."

"Yeah?" Ben raised his eyebrows.

"Yep. With your own DNA. We insert it into something called a retrovirus. You guys know what a virus is, right?"

"Like cold viruses and flu viruses?" I asked. That didn't sound like something that would make us feel better.

"Similar. Viruses are tiny organisms that infect a host cell and use it to reproduce. Retroviruses get inside a cell and then spread their *own* genetic material."

"So . . . if you have a retrovirus full of *my* genetic material . . ."

"You got it!" Dr. Ames's eyes lit up, and he nodded. "In that case, when we introduce that retrovirus to your system, we get new, healthy brain cells, reproducing to give you back what you lost. Pretty awesome, huh?" He turned and started toward the big building that I figured must be the clinic. "Now, let's continue our tour."

"Have you guys started that gene therapy yet?" I asked Sarah, who was hopping over cracks in the sidewalk.

She shook her head. "No—we're still on Phase Two. But I hope it's soon. It's totally boring here with so few kids."

"So, wait . . ." Mom rushed to catch up with Dr. Ames on the sidewalk. "You have these four, and . . . two others? Only six patients?"

"At the moment, yes. We have six *guests*." He pulled open the clinic door and held it for her. "Our numbers vary. We get people home quickly once they've recovered." He pointed down a long white hallway. "Come this way, and I'll show you the rest of the facilities."

He stopped at a set of glass doors partway down the hall. "Here's our cafeteria, where you'll have your meals unless you're having a rough day and need to eat in your room." We filed into the big, bright room. Potted plants grew along the windows, and there were four round tables that looked like regular kitchen tables in regular houses.

"Where do those steps go?" Ben asked, pointing to the staircase in the corner of the room.

"Up to the roof," Dr. Ames said. "Killer view. You can go up anytime you'd like and check it out."

"They're allowed on the *roof*?" Mom tipped her head like she'd heard wrong.

"It's more of an upstairs deck," Dr. Ames said. "Totally safe, completely fenced in." He held his hand up to his waist to show Mom how safe we'd be. "You want to see it?"

Mom looked at me.

"Not now," I said. What I really wanted was to finish this tour so I could lie down. I think Dr. Ames could tell I was starting to fade because he put an arm around Mom and led her back to the hallway.

"Our MRI and electroencephalography labs are down this way," Dr. Ames said, gesturing to his right.

"Electro-huh?" I looked down the hallway.

Dr. Ames laughed. "It's a mouthful—just a fancy name for another kind of brain scan. I'd show you, but those rooms are in use right now and I don't want to interrupt." He continued down the hallway. "Here's my office." He unlocked a door and led us into a bright, open room with a big wooden desk.

"What a lovely view," Mom said, stepping up to one of the windows that looked out over the swimming pool and, beyond that, the docks. I leaned against the desk, and my hand brushed a manila folder; there were a bunch of them, fanned out next to a laptop computer. The folders were labeled ENRIQUEZ, HAYES, JACOBS, MCCAIN, PERKINS, and mine, GRAYSON. Probably full of our medical files from home. A green Post-it note on the ENRIQUEZ folder read "Procedure Discontinued 4/18." I was wondering if that patient had already gone home, when Dr. Ames swept up all the files and dropped them into a drawer below his desk.

"Sorry about the mess. I meant to tidy up, but time gets away from me. Shall we continue?" He waited for us to leave, then pulled the door closed and locked it behind him.

"This is Dr. Gunther's office." Dr. Ames opened the next door.

This office had a smaller desk with an open laptop. Behind it, a wiry man looked up from the papers he was holding. "Oh! Hello there. I'm Dr. Gunther." He closed the laptop and pushed himself to stand. His white hair was long on the sides, combed over a bald spot on top. His face was pale and yellowy, and so were his office walls, empty except for a glass shadow box full of pinned-and-preserved butterfly specimens—one red and black, one brilliant yellow, and one glowing blue.

"Dr. Gunther is the real brains of this operation. He oversees all the treatment details," Dr. Ames said as Dr. Gunther shook our hands. His hand was papery and cold, even though the window was open, the room full of warm Florida air.

"Nice dead butterflies," Ben said. His aunt glared at him.

"Ah . . . thank you. It's a hobby of mine." Dr. Gunther hurried back to his chair and reached for his papers. His hands were all shaky.

"You're reviewing the updated files, I gather?" Dr. Ames raised his eyebrows.

"I am." Dr. Gunther sighed. "I'd like to talk with you before—"

"Later." Dr. Ames cut him off sharply, but then his voice softened. "We've got a grand tour to finish before Molly takes these folks back to the mainland." He nodded toward Ben's aunt and my mom, and I felt a twist in my stomach. I kept forgetting Mom had to leave.

"You'll want to see the guest rooms, I'm sure," Dr. Ames said, leading us back to the hallway. He paused at some big glass doors on our right. Behind them were a bunch of empty treadmills and exercise bikes. "This is the exercise therapy center," he said. "We'll have you down here in a few days, once you're ready for Phase Two of treatment."

"So soon?" Mom asked. "Cat still gets dizzy going up stairs sometimes."

Dr. Ames nodded. "Totally expected," he said, tapping the glass door with his long fingers. "But here, we introduce a very gradual exercise program, and we'll have her monitored."

"It's tough at first," Quentin said, "but it gets easier every time, and they don't push us too hard. Nothing like my football practices back home. Just enough to make you sweat a little."

"It's better than sitting around all day," Sarah added. That was easy for her to say, I thought. She hadn't stopped moving since Ben and I arrived; if she wasn't walking, she was jumping or bouncing on her toes or stretching.

"It's an important part of therapy," Dr. Ames said. "This carefully regulated return to activity helps to restore the brain's auto-regulation mechanism, if that makes sense."

"It doesn't," Ben said, leaning against the wall.

"Sorry. Here's the regular-guy version . . . When you do a cardio workout—even a mild one—it kind of resets your body's systems. That's why exercise is good for people who have been traveling and have jet lag—it helps reset the body's internal clock. And in your case . . ." He stepped right up to Ben and put a hand on his shoulder. Ben tensed but didn't pull away. ". . . that exercise will help reset your brain so it can control blood pressure and the blood supply to your brain. That can help repair the concussion damage. Now does it make more sense?"

Ben nodded. "When do we get in there?"

"Probably early next week, but you seem like a pretty fit guy. If you're feeling up to it, I'll see if we can get you started sooner. Fair enough?"

"Cool."

All this was cool, if it would really work the way he said. I was almost afraid to hope, but when I looked at Mom, she was smiling. I could tell she was imagining me running on that treadmill, maybe running along the dock at home, kayaking again.

"The other therapy room, where we do light and oxygen treatments, is just past the exercise area," Dr. Ames said, looking at his watch, "but I'd like to get you to the guest rooms so we don't run out of time. Molly has to leave soon, and she won't be making another run with the airboat tonight."

My gut twisted again. Soon, that airboat fan would roar to life and take Mom flying away over the swamp, back to Everglades City and then to the airport and Dad and home—without me. I was staying here.

"Let's see," Dr. Ames said as we followed him down another bright white hallway. "We've already got Quentin in room 104 and Sarah in 100. Cat, you'll be in 108. And my buddy Ben's in room 111. Three ones for good luck."

We got to my room first. "Welcome home, Cat." Dr. Ames opened the door to a bedroom with calm blue walls and a queen-size bed. It was cold in there—the air conditioner must have been cranked—and bright, with a window looking out at the pool and the pond.

"You've got your own bathroom here," Dr. Ames said, opening a door to reveal a sparkling clean shower, sink, and toilet. "If there's anything you need—shampoo, toothpaste—let me know and I'll send one of the orderlies." He looked at me, waiting.

"It's lovely," Mom jumped in. "Not at all like a hospital room, huh?"

"Thanks," I managed, walking to the dresser. My suitcase and backpack were already here, like Dr. Ames promised. "I guess I'll get settled."

"Absolutely," Dr. Ames said. "Let me take Ben to his room, and I'll be back in a few minutes to walk your mom back to the dock."

He pulled the door closed with a quiet click, and then it was only Mom and me. I didn't know what to say, so I started unpacking my suitcase. I put my clothes in the dresser, unwrapped the clay cardinal I brought from home, and perched her on the windowsill. I pulled out my pencil bag full of sculpting tools and the big hunk of clay I brought, all wrapped up in plastic so it wouldn't dry out. It was only enough to make three or four birds, but Mom thought it would help me pass the time, make me feel more at home. I set those on top of my dresser. Maybe I'd start a new bird later. An osprey like that one we saw.

The only thing left in my suitcase was the picture of Mom and Dad and Aunt Beth and Kathleen with Lucy and me. I pulled it out and set it up on the dresser. It was from our camping trip in the Redwoods last summer, before Lucy went to her sleepaway camp and met Mae Kim and Corinne. Before she decided she liked soccer and them better than hiking and me.

My eyes started burning, so I picked up my binoculars and went to the window. Half a dozen white birds milled around in the shallow-water weeds.

"What do you see?" Mom asked.

"Ibises, I think. They're smaller than the egrets in my bird book, and their beaks are curved."

I glanced at my watch—four thirty in Florida was one thirty at home. In an hour, Lucy would be getting out of classes, probably going for cupcakes with Corinne and Mae Kim. I wondered if she ever missed coming over after school, if she ever thought about weekends like that camping trip. We'd stayed up so late around the campfire, and Aunt Beth played her guitar, and we all sang with her. Lucy and I made up silly new lyrics for her seventies songs, and we laughed and laughed.

When I turned back to Mom, I couldn't hide the tears in my eyes.

"Oh, Cat." Mom wrapped her arms around me.

I pulled away and wiped my cheeks. "It's just . . . you know the concussion makes me all moody. I'll be fine." I said it again. "I'll be *fine*. This is where I need to be to get better."

Mom nodded, hugged me again, and didn't let go until Dr. Ames knocked on the door.

"I don't want to rush you, but Molly's down at the dock when you're ready."

"I'm ready," I said.

"Really?" Mom held me out and looked at me close, as if she could see for sure whether I was telling the truth.

I wasn't. "I'm ready," I lied again. "You can go."

She hugged me one more time. And then she left.

I didn't walk to the dock with her or even look out the window. I didn't want to go to the pool or see the roof or get to know anybody or eat dinner. All I wanted to do was sleep, so I dug through my suitcase to find my pajamas and put them on.

I flopped too hard on the bed, and my head thumped like

somebody had drumsticks whaling away inside my skull. I pressed my pillow over my ears, but it couldn't drown out the sound from the dock.

The roar of that airboat leaving with my mom on board. Leaving me here.

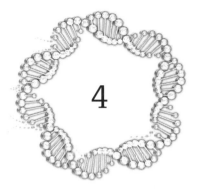

4

WHEN I WOKE, THE SUN was shining through my window, reflecting off the pond outside, making sparkle waves all over my ceiling. I blinked at the clock by my bed. Eight o'clock. If I got up now, I'd have time for breakfast before the MRI on my schedule for nine.

I sat up and braced myself for the dizziness that always came when I went from horizontal to vertical, but it didn't come.

I stood up and waited. And felt . . . weirdly okay. I turned my head to the left and right. I could tell the headache was there somewhere, behind my eyes, waiting, but it wasn't coming after me yet.

Maybe it was the medicine Dr. Ames brought me last night. He came to my door around nine with a turkey wrap, water, and two pills—my usual medicine for the headaches and something else that was supposed to increase blood flow to my brain and help repair the concussion damage. Could it be working already?

I was hungry, too, so I took a quick shower, dressed, and headed for the cafeteria.

Quentin and Sarah were side by side at a table, eating eggs and fruit. Ben sat across from them, reading *Horse and Rider* magazine. He didn't have a plate of food, only an unpeeled orange that he rolled back and forth on the table while he read.

"Oh, hi!" Sarah waved me over as if I might have a hard time spotting her through the crowd. "Sit by me. Want me to take you up to get food?"

"She can probably handle that herself," Quentin said, smiling. His smile was different from Sarah's, like he wanted to be friends but understood if I needed time to start liking him. It made me like him faster.

"Well." Sarah sounded offended. "I was just going to warn her about Elena's toast."

"Who's Elena?" I asked.

"One of the workers." Sarah pointed toward the kitchen area, where a woman with short, spiky hair was scrambling eggs. "She always burns the toast. Always. Get a bagel instead, and don't let her put it in the toaster."

That made me laugh. "Couldn't I ask her to toast it lightly?"

"She doesn't speak English. None of the helpers do." Sarah ticked them off on her fingers. "Olga and Elena and Viktor and Sergei. They're part of some medical exchange program from Russia."

"Got it," I said. "Plain bagel." I headed for the kitchen area, where a tiny buffet was set up. Elena-of-the-burned-toast was at the counter, cracking eggs into a mixing bowl.

I filled a plate with strawberries, melon, scrambled eggs with cheese, and my untoasted bagel and headed back to the table. Sarah scooted close to Ben to make room for me between her and Quentin. Ben turned away and pretended she wasn't even there.

Something about Sarah—her smile or that hey-be-my-friend look in her eyes—reminded me of Amberlee, the girl from my art class who'd tried to join our table at lunch the day I fell out of the tree stand. Lucy and Corinne had stared at her as if she'd burst into a private meeting. Amberlee stood there with her tray, swaying back and forth like a tree about to blow over in the wind. I could have moved over to make room for another chair, or I could have gone with her to a different table—I've thought a million times since then about what I could have done—but I sat there like Ben. I stared at the little cup of applesauce on my tray, and when I finally looked up, she was gone.

"So what's the deal with you guys?" Sarah asked, bringing me back from that other cafeteria. I wasn't ready to talk, so I took a bite of my eggs, then held up a finger while I chewed. She got the hint and turned to Ben. "Like, I'm from upstate New York. Way, way upstate, by Canada. Where are you from?" She gave him a nudge, and finally, he looked up from his magazine.

"Washington." He looked down and turned a page.

"DC? My hockey team went to the Smithsonian when we were there for a tournament once!"

"No."

"Oh. Washington State?"

"Yeah."

"That's cool. So how'd you get your concussion? I got checked into the boards playing hockey. This girl was absolutely huge, and she was flying. Do you play sports?"

"No."

Elena came to the table with a tray of orange juice and gave us each a glass.

"Thanks," I said. She just smiled.

Sarah poked Ben. "Well, if you don't play sports, what *do* you like?"

"Riding horses."

"I should have guessed that from your magazine, huh? Do you have a horse?"

"Yes."

"So how'd you get here?"

Ben finally looked up again. "Dude, were you not right there when we pulled up on the airboat? Or was that some other annoying skinny girl on the dock?"

"Hey," Quentin said quietly, spreading cream cheese on his untoasted bagel. "She's trying to be friendly." It should have made me happy that he was standing up for Sarah, but somehow, it made me sad. I stared at him, wondering why. "We're going to be here together a while. We might as well be friends."

Then I figured it out. Quentin was that kid I *used* to be before middle school—the one teachers chose to show new students around because they'd always be kind to kids like Amberlee. Maybe when—

"Look, this ain't summer camp." Ben slammed his magazine on the table, and his tray jumped. "I'm not here to make friends and learn archery. I'm here to get better so I can ride again."

"That's why we're all here, Mr. Personality. Besides, I wasn't asking how you *traveled* here; I was asking what happened. Like my hockey crash." She put a hand to the left side of her head as if talking about it brought back the pain. "This is my second concussion, so my doctor said no more hockey for the rest of the year at least."

"Well," I said, "this place is supposed to work wonders." I hoped it was true. For Sarah and for me. "The website makes it sound like you end up smarter than you were before your concussion."

"Yeah." Sarah let out a sharp laugh. "I think that's what my parents are hoping."

"So, um . . . Sarah already knows this. But I got hurt playing football," Quentin said.

"He's on the school team. You play quarterback, right?" The bounce in Sarah's voice was back.

"Yeah." He hesitated, then sat up a little straighter. "Quarterback."

"You get sacked or what?" Ben asked, finally peeling his orange.

"Uh, kind of. I went down pretty hard. I still get headaches, and sometimes when I'm doing my math homework, I can't remember stuff, you know? Like I'm supposed to have the information and it's probably in my brain somewhere, but it feels like everything got knocked out of place."

Sarah shrugged. "My brain always feels that way when I do math."

"What about you, Cat?" Quentin pushed his glasses up on his nose and squinted at me.

"I fell out of a tree stand." There. Embarrassing moment over. "I was watching birds up there."

I waited for them to laugh or say bird watching was an old-lady thing. But they didn't.

"Cool," Sarah said. And Quentin nodded. And then we all looked at Ben.

He took a long time chewing a section of his orange, then swallowed and said, "I . . . uh . . . fell off my horse."

"Wow," Quentin said.

"Yeah." Ben paused but then went on. "My aunt and uncle have a stable where they run programs for disabled kids. I ride there a lot." He shrugged like it was no big deal, but his face changed in a way that only happens when you're talking about something important. "I did, anyway, until I got thrown." He looked back down at his magazine, turned to a new story. And I could tell he'd told as much of *his* story as we were going to hear.

Dr. Ames came striding into the cafeteria then, jingling keys on a keychain. "Oh, good! Glad you're getting to know one another. I hate to steal you away, Cat, but you've got an MRI this morning so we can see what's going on in that head, okay?"

He walked me to the lab near his office and flicked on the lights. This room wasn't the stark white of the MRI lab at the hospital back home; it was painted a deep blue and had art prints on the walls—water lilies and meadow scenes that were probably meant to be soothing. But the most soothing thing to me was the MRI machine itself. "It's a lot more open than the one at home," I said.

Dr. Ames smiled and looked at me like he understood. "Those old models are pretty claustrophobic, aren't they? I think you'll find this more comfortable." He glanced at the clipboard in his hands. "I've got the wrong chart," he said, and gestured toward the examination table next to the MRI machine. "You can change into a robe and hop on up. I'll be right back."

He closed the door behind him, and I reached for the soft cotton robe draped over the table, but then I remembered my music. Back home, I'd get so nervous in the MRI machine it was hard for me to be still, and then they couldn't get a good scan. I'd always move and mess it up, and then I felt awful because they'd have to start over.

So Mom had the lab technicians play my favorite music—my *real* favorite music. Not Lucy's dark, moody new playlists that I listened to on the soccer bus and pretended to like. My playlists were full of happy, upbeat bands like GizMania and the Stealth Acrobats, and they helped a ton. I looked at the machine here; I'd probably be okay, but it couldn't hurt to see if I could grab my music player.

I put down the robe and opened the lab door, but Dr. Ames wasn't back yet. I looked down the hallway and saw his office door was closed, but the one next to it, Dr. Gunther's, was cracked open, with voices coming from inside.

I walked down the hall and was lifting my hand to knock, when Dr. Ames raised his voice.

"No! Not when we're so close!"

Why would he be yelling at Dr. Gunther? I lowered my hand and took half a step back.

Dr. Gunther said something I couldn't hear, and then, ". . . far enough. Think what could happen."

Dr. Ames's response came through loud and clear. "*You* think what could happen, Rudolph. Have you forgotten how we came to work together?"

I don't know if Dr. Gunther answered or if Dr. Ames kept talking over him.

"At that time, you were found to be violating federal laws that regulate genetic engineering research. At that time, you were charged with a felony. And at *that* time you were never going to set foot in a lab again. You were never going to finish your clinical research; you were never going to find your cure for Parkinson's disease. And you. Were. Going. To. Die."

That last word hung in the air. Maybe Dr. Gunther said something back, but I couldn't hear, and my thoughts were all jumbled; it happened a lot since my concussion. I could remember things from last year, but I'd forget something I heard a few minutes ago. And this . . . this was all too much to understand.

It sounded like Dr. Ames was threatening Dr. Gunther. But why? They worked together, didn't they?

Trying to sort it all out made my head hurt. I stepped back. Why was I even in this hallway? I was supposed to be in the lab having an MRI.

They were still talking in there, but only scraps of their conversation made it out the door.

". . . tumor continues to grow, and I really think . . ."

". . . better with the other first-round subject."

". . . procedure has taken, but it's early yet, and . . ."

". . . proceed as planned."

". . . must contact the girl's parents—"

"I said NO."

Dr. Ames's voice sounded so loud, so sharp, so close to the door that I jumped back, scrambled across the hall to the lab, and stumbled into the exam table. Dizzy . . . I always got dizzy when I moved too fast, and then the nausea washed over me. I put my head down and breathed in the clean detergent smell of the cotton robe until the spinning slowed and I could stand up again.

When I did, Dr. Ames was in the doorway.

"You all right, Cat? Take your time." His voice was soft again, his face concerned but not angry at all. Why was he so upset with Dr. Gunther? And did they say they were calling someone's parents? Whose? I tried to remember the conversation but it broke apart like a staticky phone call.

"Cat?" Dr. Ames stepped to my side and put a gentle hand on my arm.

"Sorry." I shook my head. "I got dizzy when I started to change."

"I see you didn't get far," he said. "Do you want Olga to come give you a hand?"

"No, that's okay." I picked up the robe and took a deep breath. "It's going away. I can get changed."

"Great," he said. "I'll be outside; give a knock when you're ready."

The door closed, and I concentrated on moving slowly, smoothly, so I didn't jar myself dizzy again. I concentrated on the feel of the cotton and the smell of the lab. On everything but the words I couldn't sort out, because my head felt foggy every time I tried.

I knocked on the door. "I'm ready."

Dr. Ames came back with his clipboard. "Great. Climb on up."

I hoisted myself onto the exam table and leaned back.

"Relax and let your arms rest at your sides, okay? You want some music?"

"What?" The words made my heart jump, and I leaned up on my elbows. I never told Dr. Ames I wanted to go get music. Had he seen me in the hallway? No, he couldn't have known. I didn't even mention it. And why was I so scared that he might know I was in the hallway? Somehow, even though the words didn't make sense to me yet, I knew I'd heard something I shouldn't have.

"I asked if you wanted music." Dr. Ames was standing by a computer on the counter. "Some of our patients find that music makes it easier to relax for the MRI. I've got some light jazz, a bunch of classic rock . . . Bruce Springsteen, Journey . . . I'm probably dating myself, huh?" He grinned and shrugged. "Sorry I can't offer you something more current."

"No, that's okay," I said, settling on the exam table. "Classic rock is fine. Everything's fine."

Maybe it was, I thought.

Dr. Ames flipped a switch on the wall, and my table moved slowly toward the scanner that was going to take pictures of my brain.

Everything had to be fine. I pushed the echoing words I'd overheard down into the shadows of my head and took a deep breath.

Everything was fine. These were doctors, after all, and this was where I needed to be to get better. I had to trust them.

5

"ALL DONE FOR TODAY. THAT was painless, wasn't it?" Dr. Ames leaned against the counter and turned off the music.

"It's way better than the one at home," I said. "What do I do the rest of the morning?"

He looked out the window. "It's a beautiful day. Maybe take a swim or read a book by the pool?"

"I mean, do I have more tests or treatments or anything?" I leaned over to peek at the papers on his clipboard.

"Nope, nothing else today. Phase One of treatment is simply getting you settled, getting the daily brain scans, making sure we have your meds right. We'll begin light, oxygen, and exercise therapies soon, though. And you can see this anytime you want, by the way. It's your chart." He handed me the clipboard.

Name: Catherine Grayson
Age: 12
IQ: 132

Mother: Anne Woods Grayson—Age 52
Father: Robert Grayson—Age 55
Siblings: None
Family Medical History: Heart attack—paternal grandfather
Concussion Report: Subject sustained damage to right frontal lobe
    of brain after falling from playhouse in tree.
Risk Level: Moderate

Below that were a bunch of boxes for dates and vital signs
heart rate and blood pressure and stuff, as well as space for notes
on MRIs and treatments.

"I'm always happy to answer questions, Cat. This is *your*
treatment, and you should know exactly what's going on."

"Thanks." I felt like I should have lots of questions, but I
couldn't sort them out. I stared down at the chart. The word "risk"
jumped out from the paper. "What does 'risk level' mean?"

"That's . . . risk is really the wrong word for it. It's an assess-
ment of how severe your injury was when you came here, and
yours was merely moderate—nothing life-threatening, even though
we understand that the post-concussion symptoms have changed
the way you do things from day to day."

"Oh." I looked back down at the paper. It didn't quite make
sense, but I was getting tired. The numbers and letters were starting to blur.

"Anything else, Cat?" Dr. Ames raised his eyebrows and
smiled.

There was something else. I'd wanted to tell him that I fell
from a tree stand for bird watching . . . not a playhouse. Playhouse

made me sound like I was eight years old. But I couldn't find the words, and looking all over my head for them was hard. "No. That's it, I guess."

"Great. So here are your morning meds. I'll trade you. . . ." He took back my chart and handed me a little cup with two pills and a bigger cup full of water. I swallowed the pills and tossed the cups in the trash.

Dr. Ames held open the lab door and pointed me in the direction of the hallway that led outside. "Why don't you get some fresh air? I bet Sarah and Quentin will be happy to see you."

"Okay." I started down the hall, but I didn't go outside. I went back to my room, thinking about Sarah and Quentin and the other girl who was supposed to be here and the boy Sarah seemed to like even though he was blowing her off. Brett? Brent? Which kid's parents were the doctors talking about calling?

"Hey, there you are!" Sarah's bouncy voice was like a jack-hammer to my muddled head. She hurried down the hall before I could step into my room and disappear back into bed. "We need you for Frisbee!"

"Maybe later," I said, leaning against the wall. Across from me, Sarah's room had a folder on the door with a chart that looked like mine from the lab. "Does that tell how you got hurt and everything?" I asked her, pointing to it.

"Probably." She shrugged. "But I already told you that. I got checked into the boards playing hockey."

"Sorry." I kind of remembered. "I still forget stuff."

Sarah nodded and reached for her chart. "That'll get better when you start the second phase of treatment. See?" She held it out and pointed to the activity log on the bottom. "I've already had two weeks of light and oxygen therapy and exercise. My headaches are pretty much gone."

"Well, that explains the Frisbee," I said, and looked down at her chart.

Name: Sarah L. Jacobsen
Age: 12
IQ: 98
Mother: Loree Elizabeth Martin—Age 38
Father: John Jacobsen—Age 38
Siblings: Kurt Jacobsen—Age 15
Family Medical History: Cancer—maternal grandmother
Concussion Report: Subject suffered damage to right frontal lobe of
   brain while playing hockey.
Risk Level: Moderate

"Hey, your injury was to the same part of your brain as mine, I think." I pointed to that part of the chart. "And your risk level, too."

"What's that?" She leaned over to look.

"It's . . . like how bad your injury was." I couldn't believe she'd been here two weeks and hadn't read her chart yet. But now Sarah was going from door to door, collecting everyone's—even two way down at the end of the hall. They must have belonged to the kids I hadn't met yet.

"Well, that's weird," Sarah said. "Trent's injury was way worse than mine—he told me he was unconscious for like half an hour—and his risk level is low. So is Ben's and that horse accident sounded serious, didn't it?"

"Maybe it was a different kind of injury or something," I said, opening my door. I didn't want to talk anymore.

"No, because look." Sarah wedged herself between me and my door and held up the chart.

Name: Ben McCain
Age: 14
IQ: 108
Mother: Vonna Sterling McCain—Deceased
Father: Francis James McCain—Deceased
Uncle: Andrew F. McCain—45
Aunt: Wendy Erwin McCain—35
Siblings: None
Family Medical History: Depression, mental illness—maternal
    grandmother
Concussion Report: Subject was thrown from horse, suffered
    concussion to right frontal lobe of brain.
Risk Level: Low

"See? It's his right frontal lobe, like ours," Sarah said. "And so is Quentin's! And Trent's. And Kaylee's, too! That is so weird." She flipped through the other charts and handed them to me.

Name: Quentin R. Hayes
Age: 13
IQ: 130

Mother: Jacqueline Marshfield Hayes—Age 40

Father: Robert M. Hayes—Age 48

Siblings: Christopher Hayes—Age 9

Family Medical History: Heart disease—maternal grandmother, paternal grandfather and uncle

Concussion Report: Subject hit head on ground while playing football. Injury is to right frontal lobe. Post-concussion symptoms have included disorientation, headaches, inability to concentrate.

Risk Level: Moderate to high

Name: Trent Perkins

Age: 13

IQ: 110

Mother: Mary Ann Perkins—Deceased

Father: Jake Perkins—Deceased

Contact: Ronald and Mabel Inman, foster parents

Siblings: Jason Perkins—Age 5

Family Medical History: Heart attack—paternal grandmother; lung cancer—maternal grandfather

Concussion Report: Subject sustained damage to right frontal lobe of the brain after being knocked down on basketball court.

Risk Level: Low

Name: Kaylee Enriquez

Age: 12

IQ: 122

Mother: Tracy Roberts Enriquez—Age 35

Father: John Enriquez—Age 40

Siblings: None

Family Medical History: Stroke—maternal grandmother

Concussion Report: Subject suffered damage to right frontal lobe
of brain after falling from bicycle.

Risk Level: Low to Medium

"That is so weird," Sarah said again.

"What's weird?" Quentin asked, coming down the hall with Ben.

"Well, we were looking at your charts—"

"*She* was looking at your charts." I knew Ben would be angry. "I was going to take a nap."

"Geez," Ben said, yanking the folders from Sarah's hands. He glanced down, then put each one back on the door of its owner. "You been in my room, looking through my underwear drawer, too?"

"You wish," Sarah said. "Seriously, though . . . if you look at those charts, all our injuries are to the same part of our brains—the right frontal lobe."

"That's the part of the brain that deals with problem solving and divergent thinking," Quentin said.

"What are you, Encyclopedia Boy?" Ben said.

Quentin looked down at his sneakers. "No. I was in Science Olympiad last year, and one of my events was Human Anatomy and Physiology. Anyway," he said, turning to Sarah. "It's probably a common kind of head injury is all."

"Yeah, but don't you think it's fishy?" Sarah pushed.

"Fishy?" Quentin shook his head, laughing. "No. And don't

go all conspiracy-theory on me again." He turned to Ben and me. "She was a mess when we first got here—completely wigged out. Like, what if we don't get better? What if these guys are really kidnappers or something? What if—"

"Quit it." Sarah's voice was sharp. "I thought . . . and I still think . . . some things here are weird. Just because we got forced to come doesn't mean we have to be good little patients and never ask questions."

"I didn't get forced to come," I said. "I wanted to come."

"Me, too." Quentin picked up his file and looked at it. "If I don't get better, my whole future's out the window. My mom was psyched when Dr. Ames found us."

"Yeah, my parents, too." Sarah rolled her eyes. "They're going to be ticked off if I don't come back smarter, though."

"Wait . . . Dr. Ames found *you*?" I asked.

"Yeah. He told my mom he has to keep a certain number of patients to keep his research grant, so they network with hospitals all over the country and recruit kids they think have a good chance of a positive outcome. That's not what happened with you?"

"No. My mom found the clinic online."

"Well, it doesn't really matter," Sarah said. "We're all here now, and we might as well make the best of it." She held up her Frisbee. "Who's in for a game before lunch?"

Quentin smiled at me and shrugged. My headache was fading—the new meds really did seem to work better—so I followed them out to the lawn.

We had only tossed the Frisbee around for a few minutes before Ben missed catching an easy toss from Quentin and threw up his hands. "I'm done," he said, and plopped himself down in a lawn chair by the pool.

"Me, too. I'm tired." I headed for the pool and sank down in the chair next to Ben. He was reading again, so I didn't say anything—people who talk while you're reading are the worst. I watched the ibises, poking their beaks into the shallow water of the pond.

"Your head hurt?" Ben asked, looking up from his magazine.

"Kind of." I nodded toward Quentin and Sarah. "They say it goes away once the next phase of treatment starts."

"Hope it goes fast," he said quietly.

"I know. I miss my mom and dad like crazy." The words slipped out before I remembered the word next to his parents' names on the chart: *deceased*.

"Me, too," he said with a sad laugh.

"I . . . sorry."

"It's okay," he said. "I mean, it's not, but . . ." He shrugged. "It's been a while now. I've lived with my aunt and uncle two years."

I watched Sarah and Quentin running over the grass. I thought Ben would go back to his magazine, but he didn't. "My mom died when I was really little. And then my dad got killed in Afghanistan."

"Hey, you guys ready to get back in the game?" Sarah came running up, her face all red and sweaty. Quentin was behind her with the Frisbee. "What are you talking about over here?"

Ben looked up at her. "My dead parents," he said, his voice flat.

"Oh . . . I . . ." For once, Sarah didn't have something to say.

And again, standing there, she reminded me of Amberlee. "I'm sorry. I didn't know."

"Really?" Ben gave her a mocking look of surprise. "It was on my *chart*."

I didn't want to pick a fight with Ben, but I felt bad for Sarah. She was stuck here like the rest of us.

"Was your dad in the military?" I asked Ben.

"Yeah." Ben sat up a little straighter. "Marines."

"I bet you're close to the rest of your family, huh?" Quentin asked, pulling up a chair.

Ben's right eye twitched. "Yeah. My aunt and uncle are okay. How about you, Encyclopedia Boy?"

Quentin smiled. "I guess I can live with that nickname. I do study a lot. My family expects me to get a scholarship."

Sarah made a face. "Who cares what they expect?"

"I do," Quentin said right away. He looked down at the Frisbee, passing it from hand to hand. "My mom and dad work hard so they'll be able to send me to college. Mom's a teacher. Dad's a police officer, and he's always pulling extra shifts. And my grandparents—they aren't around anymore—but they were amazing people, too. Grandpa had a restaurant where everybody in town went for breakfast—professors and politicians—Barack Obama even ate there sometimes. Grandpa let me help put out napkins and stuff. He made everybody feel important, whether you were the richest guy on the block or a homeless lady looking for a cup of coffee. And Grandma Jo . . . she lived in Alabama in the sixties, during the bus boycotts, and she marched in Birmingham. She had a picture with Martin Luther King and everything."

"Wow! My aunt Beth would have loved her. She and Kathleen are always protesting something—discrimination or cutting down trees or whatever. Aunt Beth says she wants to leave the world a better place for me."

Ben smirked. "That's cheesy." The word stung. Lucy had said the same thing and rolled her eyes when I invited her to Aunt Beth's canvas-the-city recycling rally in September. I ended up not going either.

"Well, I think it's pretty awesome," Quentin said. "Anyway, before my grandma died, she used to call me every quarter when report cards came out. I don't know how she knew, but man . . . I'd better have done my best. She said she didn't get the snot beat out of her on a dusty road so I could hang around getting Cs." He sighed. "When I got hurt, I couldn't think as fast. It's like the part of my brain that used to solve problems got busted. But it feels like it's finally starting to come back."

"Be lucky you had it at all." Sarah laughed. She reached for the Frisbee and stood up, but then paused and looked at Quentin. "Tell me this. If this is really such a great clinic, how come there's nobody here? And where are Kaylee and Trent? We never see either of them anymore."

"Maybe *aliens* abducted them!" Ben leaned forward in his chair and used his hands to make wiggling antennas over his ears.

Quentin laughed. "Or giant alligators."

"Giant *alien* alligators!" Ben said, giving Quentin a high five. "You want to get something to drink?" They headed for the building, and Sarah sighed and started after them. I did, too, but not without looking back at those perfect, empty lawn chairs. Why *was* it so quiet here?

I still couldn't piece together what I'd heard standing outside the office, but a part of my mind wouldn't stay quiet, no matter how many times I told myself everything was okay.

6

I SPENT THE REST OF the morning in my room, trying to work on a bird. I unwrapped my clay and breathed in big gulps of its earthy smell, and if I closed my eyes, I could almost believe I was home, in my room, with the cool clay in my hands and all my birds sitting on their painted branches, watching over my bed. When I opened my eyes and squeezed the clay, nothing worked. The picture in my book captured the power and strength of that osprey by the docks so perfectly. But the clay in my hands was brittle and weak. I tried three or four times before I crushed the whole thing into a lumpy ball and wrapped it back up with the rest.

Then I flopped down on my bed and tried to read a little. Mom had convinced me to bring a few of my favorite historical novels and some book my English class read while I was absent. It was about a girl who finds a magic bread box, which sounds weird, but Mrs. Rock said I'd like it. I tried the first chapter, but within a couple paragraphs, the words were swirling out of focus.

Nothing was right here. I tossed the book on the floor, and

the clunk it made hurt my head. It was time for my meds, and time for lunch, too, so I headed down the hallway to the cafeteria.

Ben was reading another magazine and wolfing down a turkey sandwich as if he'd never had a meal so good, and Sarah was blabbing away at Quentin. I ate my chicken salad and watched a great blue heron hunting in the pond out the window. It spent forever stalking a frog before it finally jabbed its beak into the water and caught it. I tried to imagine how I'd shape the heron in clay, but all I could see in my mind was another frustrated lump.

We all looked up when the door opened and Dr. Gunther shuffled into the dining room, looking even older than he had at his desk that first day.

Ben whispered what I was thinking. "This is the miracle neurologist who's supposed to cure us?"

"Hi, Dr. Gunther." Quentin gave a wave as Dr. Gunther stepped up to our table.

"Hello, indeed. I came by to see how our newest guests are doing." His smile, all thin lips and yellow teeth, didn't make me feel good about being his patient. But he was looking right at me.

"I'm doing . . . okay, I guess. Nothing's really started yet."

He nodded. "We'll get things moving for you soon, though, and then you'll see real improvement. Sarah and Quentin have only been with us a couple of weeks and are already doing better, isn't that right?"

Sarah nodded reluctantly. "I guess."

"My headaches are gone," Quentin said, "and I'm thinking more clearly. But it still takes me too long to process math problems."

Sarah stole a carrot stick off his plate. "Those of us who don't do math problems for fun aren't having that issue."

Dr. Gunther laughed and turned to Quentin. "You'll notice a big change when we start Phase Three."

I still didn't get how the gene therapy worked. "Is that like a pill or . . ."

"An injection," Dr. Gunther answered.

The look on my face must have given away how I felt about needles.

"Relax," Dr. Gunther said. "It's not happening today, my dear. And besides, it's a piece of cake. You can ask our friend Trent."

That's when I noticed the other kid, sitting two tables over, half-hidden behind a potted plant. Maybe he snuck in while Dr. Gunther was talking, or maybe he'd been there all along, eyes cast down at his hands, studying something—was it colored yarn? Wires?—wrapped around his fingers. His blond hair was short on the sides but shaggy on top and brushed to one side. He had a bandage on the back of his head, and it looked like the hair around that spot had been shaved. I wondered if that was part of his treatment.

"Hey!" Sarah jumped right up and ran to his table. "Where have you been?"

Trent looked up. "I'm sorry?" He looked as if he'd just realized he wasn't in the room alone and seemed completely unraveled.

I felt bad for him. "Hi. I'm Cat," I said, holding out my hand. "I'm new here, but Sarah's told me a lot about you. It's nice to meet you." Trent looked at my hand without shaking it, then looked back at Sarah.

"Sarah?" he said as if he couldn't quite place her. "I'm sorry. I was working on reversing this current. What did you say before?"

Sarah looked at him, bewildered. "I *said* where have you been? You totally blew me off when we were supposed to shoot hoops."

"Hoops?"

"Hoops. Basketball. You were going to meet me the other night so we could play on the court outside after dinner? Where'd you go?"

Trent's eyes brightened for a second, as if he remembered, but just as quickly, the light went out and he just looked confused. "I've been taking most of my meals in the workshop lately." He shrugged. "I apologize if I neglected an appointment, but I'm quite close to understanding an important theory of alternating currents."

"What?" Sarah looked as if she might punch him, but Dr. Gunther stepped between them.

"If I might answer for Trent," he said, "Phase Three of treatment is effective because it's intense. He's been extremely busy not only with treatments but also with returning to his old passions. He wasn't quite himself when he arrived with his injury. Isn't that right?" Dr. Gunther put a shaky hand on Trent's shoulder.

Trent nodded briskly, then looked longingly back to the wires in his hands.

"I see you're focused on your experiment." Dr. Gunther smiled down at Trent. "Feel free to take the rest of your lunch down to the workshop if you'd like."

"I think I'll do that, yes."

"What workshop?" Sarah squinted at them. "We never saw any workshop."

Dr. Gunther brushed off her question. "Just a small space we've set up so Trent can pursue his projects."

Sarah turned to Trent. "Since when are you Mr. Science Geek? You never talked about any projects before." Trent frowned at her for a second, then picked up his sandwich and headed for the door.

Dr. Gunther watched him leave, then turned toward the rest of us. "Trent has always loved engineering but lost the mental capacity for it when he was injured. We're making sure he has plenty of opportunities to tinker now that he's getting back to his old self."

"His old self?" Sarah's voice rose, challenging Dr. Gunther. "He never said anything about that to me."

Dr. Gunther ignored her and turned to Quentin. "Like you, Trent was having trouble with problem solving after his accident, but ever since Phase Three of his treatment, he's doing much better. We're so pleased with his progress." Dr. Gunther glanced down at his watch. His hand shook. "I'd best get back to work."

He shuffled across the room and out the doors, headed toward his office.

We all watched him, and finally, Sarah said, "He wasn't like that before."

"Dr. Gunther?" I asked.

"No. Trent." She turned to Quentin. "Don't you think he's different?"

Quentin shrugged. "I never talked with him that much." He grinned at Sarah. "You kind of monopolized the guy's time."

"But he wasn't like that." She stared at the door as if the real Trent might come walking back through any second. "Trent was . . . goofy and fun. He liked the New York Knicks and those silly, stupid horror movies and . . . and *bacon.* Not all this *science* stuff." She shook her head. "He always had a ton of energy. Even when he hadn't gone through much treatment and he still had headaches and stuff, we shot baskets and played H-O-R-S-E, and he used to tease me about being so skinny, even though I always beat him."

"Sounds like he got tired of you," Ben said.

"That's not it. Trent was . . . he was *nice* before. And funny. He'd make these volcanoes out of his mashed potatoes and gravy at dinner. One time we got laughing so hard, milk came right out his nose, and—"

"So, he used to act like a five-year-old?" Ben scoffed. "Sounds like his treatment's working, and he's not a doofus now." He looked at Sarah. "No wonder he can't relate to you."

The words stung *me,* so I could only imagine how Sarah felt. I couldn't find the right words in my head to fix it, though, so I didn't say anything.

But Quentin did. "Come on, man." He put a hand on Ben's arm. "Ease up." He turned to Sarah. "Trent's probably tired. You spend a lot more hours in the lab with Phrase Three; I bet he's wiped out."

"Then why does he have the energy to go off to some lab and do experiments? He never told me *anything* about wanting to be an engineer. I'm telling you, he's *different.*"

"Because he's not into you anymore?" Ben said, giving her a pointed look.

"Come on, you guys," Quentin said, standing. "It's nice out. Let's hang by the pool or something."

We all followed him out there. Sarah flopped down and kicked her feet in the water, while Ben and Quentin chose chairs in the shade of a table umbrella. I stood near the trunk of a big white pine next to the clinic. I'd noticed an osprey nest, a mess of sticks and grass way up at the top.

The nest was quiet, but my insides were fluttering all over the place. What if Sarah's crazy ideas weren't so crazy? What if Trent's treatment really had changed him somehow? He didn't seem like a normal kid.

When I looked over the pool, the sun flickered through palm trees, throwing diamond sparkles all over the water's surface.

Another perfect day. A state-of-the-art research facility and clinic with top-notch care.

The best in the world, the brochure promised. And no waiting list to get in? When Lucy's grandmother had cancer, she waited months to get into some elite clinic in New York City. If this place was the best of the best for head injuries, why were we the only ones here?

7

MY SCHEDULE WASN'T MUCH OF a schedule while I waited for the next phase of treatment to begin. The rest of my day was empty, but I felt too muddled to work on a clay bird, and I didn't feel like reading.

Sarah had gone out kayaking with Quentin, and Ben had another MRI, so before dinner, I took my binoculars and headed for that narrow staircase off the dining room that led up to the roof.

I was a little worried about the height, but Dr. Ames had promised on the first day it was all fenced in and safe, and I really wanted to know if there were babies in that nest. Maybe a mom or a dad would come to feed them. And maybe seeing another osprey would make it easier when I picked up my clay again.

I clutched the railing and focused on each step, one at a time, all the way up.

It wasn't even noon yet, but a wave of hot-tar smell blasted my face as soon as I opened the door at the top of the stairs. Heat waves rose from the rooftop and blurred the scrubby pine trees in the distance.

The surface burned through my flip-flop soles as I started toward the far railing near the nest. It was high, and my heart was beating in my throat. *Keep walking; it's perfectly safe.*

If I was ever going to do anything fun again without being scared of falling, I had to start sometime. And the small tastes of life-without-headaches that I was getting with my new meds made me want my old life back more than ever.

I watched my feet—one step at a time, slowly, one foot in front of the other—and didn't look up until I reached the railing.

My knees wobbled, but I took a deep breath and willed myself to look up.

Up at the nest. Not down.

It was higher than the roof, higher than I could really see, but I held on to the railing, my heart shivering in my chest, and watched. I could hear the mother osprey rustling around. I shifted my weight from foot to foot, but the heat and the tar smell got to be too much. My head was starting to hurt, and my breakfast felt sour in my stomach. I'd have to look for hatchlings some other time, when I felt better, when the sun wasn't so hot.

As I was turning for the door, there was a high-pitched "*Eep! Eep! Eeeep!*" The mama bird was standing right up in that nest, yelling. *At me?*

I turned back and watched her watch me, and somehow, that slowed my heart, soothed my stomach and my nerves. After a few minutes, two little heads popped up at the side of the nest.

Slowly—I didn't want to upset her again—I raised my binoculars to see the babies more clearly. I was expecting soft and cuddly, but what I saw through the lenses were hooked-beak, yellow-eyed, yeeping creatures that looked more like scrawny baby dinosaurs than birds. Their feathers weren't fluffy; they were matted and stuck to their heads, and the babies were shrieking, "*Eep! Eeep!*"

I stepped forward to the railing and glanced down for a second.

I shouldn't have. The ground was so far away it made my stomach twist and my head spin. The air felt so hot, so smothering, I thought I might pass out.

I held the railing tight and looked for a place to get out of the sun. There was only a tiny column of shade cast by one of the exhaust pipes rising up from the kitchen, so I shuffled over to it and crouched down in the relative cool.

The birds were still screaming at me, but I tried to block everything out. *Breathe. Breathe. You're okay. Just breathe.*

It's a wonder I could hear it over the osprey chorus, but I did. The door to the roof creaked, and then came a man's voice. "Yeah . . . I'm here. Hang on." It was Dr. Ames. The door slammed. "Okay, now what?"

I peeked around the edge of the exhaust pipe and saw the back of Dr. Ames's head, cell phone pressed to his ear as he tipped back and forth from his heels to his toes, looking out over the swamp. They told us our cell phones wouldn't work here; we had to make all our calls from the offices. But *his* phone seemed fine—he'd used it out by the pool, too, on the day we arrived. Did he have some kind of special satellite connection?

I knew I should come out from the shadows and say hi, let him know I was there, but it already felt weird . . . like he'd think I was hiding. Spying on him. So I stayed where I was and listened.

"I don't know how long we can keep it quiet. I talked to Gunther, and he . . . yeah. I know."

A breeze ruffled the pine tree, and the mama osprey flew off.

"I told him what we decided a long time ago. This project gets finished. No matter what."

Pause.

"Exactly."

Pause.

"So what's the plan if she dies here?"

I was leaning against a sun-warmed pipe, but his question made me shiver. If *who* dies here? Was one of us in such bad shape that might happen? It couldn't be me or Sarah—but we hadn't seen that Kaylee girl around. Quentin said her injury was more serious.

All the anxiety that had lifted from me watching the birds came back, twisting my stomach, pounding on my head from the inside. Now I *had* to stay hidden; somehow, I knew I was hearing something I shouldn't.

A wave of nausea hit me. I held my breath and squeezed my eyes. *No. Don't get sick. He'll hear you. Don't get sick.*

"Well, hopefully it doesn't come to that. We're close. The new genes are establishing nicely in the Perkins boy, and he shows no signs of tumor growth. We did the implant last night, and everything's progressing as it should."

Tumor growth . . . The Perkins boy . . . That had to be Trent, the kid from breakfast. *New genes?* Sarah said he was different from before. And what was *the implant*? Thoughts fired like machine guns in my head. There was no time to pull them together.

"Much better, yes. We're moving ahead."

The mama osprey called again, and I opened my eyes. She was circling overhead. I don't think she trusted either of us on this roof.

"We'll finish with the next two kids and then speed things up—do Phase Two and Phase Three together—for the new ones. They're good candidates for the procedure so it should be fine. . . . I told Gunther we need to move on this. I'd say . . . what's today, Wednesday? Figure by Monday, we'll have four more subjects undergoing the change."

Change? It wasn't how most people would describe treatment for a concussion.

"Okay. Sounds good."

Unless . . .

"Yeah, I will. Bye."

What if . . .

I stayed on the roof while he walked back to the door and climbed down the stairs, and I felt it in my body, more than thought it.

What if Sarah was right?

And something at I-CAN was horribly, dangerously wrong.

8

"I WANT TO CALL MY mom." I knocked on the half-open door and blurted the words at the same time. Mom fixed everything. She could fix this if something was wrong or, more likely, bring me back from my crazy ideas and remind me everything was okay.

Dr. Ames put down the MRI scan he'd been studying. "How come, Cat? You feeling okay?" He tipped his head, looked at me from across his desk, and my throat got all tight. He couldn't have known that I was on the roof. I'd waited until he finished his conversation, until he was gone, and then counted to a hundred to make sure he wasn't coming back.

"I'm fine." I wasn't really. I was hot and thirsty and dizzy and confused and . . . "I'm homesick. I need to talk to my mom."

"Of course. You know you can call home anytime." He smiled, handed me the cordless phone from his desk, and motioned to the chair opposite him. "Have a seat," he said. "I need to finish reviewing these scans. Pretend I'm not even here."

I dialed with shaky fingers. What could I say? Something felt wrong. But I couldn't explain what—I didn't know. All those bits of conversations . . . My head hurt, and I couldn't pull them together to explain, and I couldn't even *try* to do that with Dr. Ames sitting across from me.

"Hello?"

"Hi, Mom."

"Cat, honey! Everything okay?"

Dr. Ames looked up from his papers for a second. Could he hear her side of the conversation, too?

"Yeah . . . fine."

Why was my chest so tight? What *was* it I'd heard up on the roof? He had called our treatment "the change," but so what? Fixing something broken was changing it. Suddenly, the phone seemed heavy in my hand, and I felt like a whiny little kid. "Everything's fine, Mom." I was being ridiculous, sucked into Sarah's nervous theories. And I didn't want to worry Mom. "I missed you today, is all. It's good to hear your voice."

It was. I took a deep breath. Whatever Dr. Ames was talking about on the roof, there had to be an explanation. He was a *doctor* who'd spent his whole life working to help kids like me.

Another snatch of conversation drifted through the mess in my head. *If she dies here . . .*

But this was a health clinic where some kids had serious injuries. As scary as it was to think about, it made sense that not all of them would be okay. My head injury wasn't like that, though. I was going to be fine. Better than fine.

"Cat? You still there?"

"Yeah. Sorry."

"So, how are the Florida birds?"

"Great. There are . . ." I was going to tell her about the osprey babies, how they looked like little dinosaurs, but if I did, Dr. Ames would know I'd been on the roof. "I love watching them in the pond from my window." Dr. Ames drifted back to his papers. "Anyway, I'm settling in and wanted to say hi. I'll let you get going."

"All right. Love you. I'll talk to you soon."

"Love you, too. Bye."

I handed the phone back to Dr. Ames. "Thanks."

"No problem. Everything okay?"

I nodded. "Yep."

Maybe it was.

I took my binoculars and headed to the pool. Quentin waved to me on his way inside. "Time for another MRI. I'll catch you at lunch."

Sarah was sprawled in a deck chair. I wasn't going to say anything about what I heard, but she took off her sunglasses to look at me. "Where were you just now?"

"On the roof." My heart sped up. "I went up to see that osprey nest." I pointed to the tree. The mama bird was back at her post now.

"Oh." Sarah sounded disappointed. "I thought maybe you decided we should check things out."

"Like what?"

"Like what happened to Trent."

I sighed. "Is he really that different?"

"You have no idea." Her eyes filled with quick, shiny tears.

She swiped them away and leaned in closer to me. "Quentin doesn't even know this, and I really don't want Ben to know, but we were kind of . . . going out, I think."

"Going out where?" The clinic wasn't exactly full of places to have dates.

"Not going anywhere, but like . . . getting to be boyfriend and girlfriend. At least I thought we were. I told you how much fun we had in the cafeteria—I don't care if Ben thinks it's dumb—it was *fun*, and it felt good to finally laugh here. And then the other night, we were sitting on the dock talking after dinner. He told me about Jason, his little brother who has Down syndrome, and how he was teaching him how to play basketball, and then he put his hand down kind of on top of mine, and I thought it was an accident, but then we were holding hands." She sighed. "And then he wasn't around the next day."

"Until breakfast this morning?"

"Yeah." She shook her head. "And you saw him there. It was like he didn't even know me."

I wasn't going to tell her. But bits of conversation from the roof kept bobbing to the surface in my brain.

If she dies here . . .

Undergoing the change . . .

If I said it out loud, sorted it out, maybe it would make sense. There had to be an explanation.

So I tried to explain what I'd heard on the roof. It came out in mismatched phrases and all out of order, but I tried to remember the important parts. I told her about the snatches of conversation I'd heard coming from Dr. Gunther's office, too.

Sarah's eyes got huge. "See? I *knew* something wasn't right.

We have to find out more. We need to—" She stopped talking and craned her neck, looking across the pool. Ben was over on the lawn playing ladder golf by himself. Dr. Gunther was shuffling toward the airboat, where Sawgrass Molly waited to take him into town or somewhere. Out here, the river was the only road.

"Where's Quentin?" she asked.

"He's got an MRI with Dr. Ames before lunch."

"That's perfect." Sarah stood up and pulled on a big T-shirt over her swimsuit. "Come on. Dr. Ames will be busy with the MRI for a while, and Dr. Gunther's leaving." I followed her gaze down by the dock. Dr. Gunther climbed into the airboat and settled on a seat. Molly waved to us as the engine growled to life, and they started down the river toward town. "Let's go," Sarah said.

"Go where?"

"Dr. Ames's office!" Her dark eyes danced. To her, this was some big adventure, like sneaking into the other team's locker room.

"What do you think we'll find?" Part of me was sure we wouldn't find anything, sure that I must have heard wrong or misunderstood. But part of me was afraid—terrified—we'd find evidence Sarah was right . . . and something was wrong.

"I don't know. We'll just"—she waved her hand through the air—"we'll do what they do on those TV lawyer shows and poke around his computer. Come with me. If nothing's going on . . . if we're wrong about that—"

"If *you're* wrong," I corrected her.

"Fine." She tossed her towel over her shoulder and tapped her foot, waiting for me to stand up. "If *I'm* wrong, then at the very least, maybe we'll get to read some juicy e-mails from his girlfriend or something." She grinned.

"Eww!" I got up and followed her, laughing. It helped me pretend, all the way down the long hallway to Dr. Ames's office, that we were really there to snoop for juicy e-mails.

"Shoot." Sarah jiggled the door handle. "It's locked." She hopped down the hall to the next door, already ajar—"But this one's not!"—and pushed it open. The room was warm, the window open again, and afternoon sun reflected off Dr. Gunther's name-plate on the desk. I stepped inside and paused. My stomach twisted.

"Sarah, maybe this isn't a good idea." I tried to make light of it. "I mean, think about Dr. Gunther. Who would write *him* juicy e-mails?"

"Ha!" She slipped behind the desk.

"Seriously, what if they catch us?"

"Dr. Gunther's going to be gone a while; you don't get any-where fast in the swamp. And Dr. Ames must be settled in the lab by now."

"What if he comes back?" My own voice echoed in my ears. Pain was building behind my eyes. Just a little, but I knew another headache was coming. I squeezed my eyes shut.

When I opened them, Sarah was poking at the computer on Dr. Gunther's desk. "Let's see . . . ," she said, clicking the mouse.

Even with the window open, Dr. Gunther's office smelled like an old man—all stale breath and antique books. I walked to the window and took a deep gulp of fresh air. I couldn't believe I'd broken into this office with her. All I'd wanted was to come to the clinic and get better. What if we got caught? And sent home? I'd have headaches forever. I'd never get my old life back. "Sarah, this is dumb."

"Hold on. I want to see what's here."

I leaned against the shelf under the windows, and my eyes fell on the huge frame of butterflies on the wall.

Aunt Beth and Kathleen gave me a butterfly field guide when they took me to tag monarchs last year, and I recognized one of Dr. Gunther's butterflies as a blue morpho. Next to it was an even bigger butterfly, with a bright yellow body and shining green-blue-black wings. Aunt Beth had pointed that one out to me in the book—the Queen Alexandra's Birdwing—because it's endangered.

"That big one's gorgeous," Sarah said, glancing up from the computer.

"It's rare, too," I said. "I'm pretty sure it's supposed to be protected."

Sarah walked past the butterflies to some framed photographs closer to the door. "Whoa! Look at Dr. Gunther in this one; he used to have actual hair and not that bad comb-over."

The photograph showed a ribbon-cutting ceremony for I-CAN four years ago, when it first opened. I recognized the front entryway. Dr. Ames was there, standing next to some older guy in a three-piece suit. He had the scissors for the ribbon cutting and must have been important. Dr. Gunther stood across from them, a strained look on his face. Sarah was right; he did have more hair back then.

I turned back to the butterflies too fast and felt so dizzy I had to reach out for the wall. "Sarah, let's go."

"Come see this first." She hurried back to the desk and turned the computer monitor toward me.

Dr. Gunther only had three folders next to the hard drive icon on his screen: Video Feed, Subjects, and Research.

"This Video Feed folder is full of dated video files." Sarah clicked on one from earlier this week, and a grainy image of the empty swimming pool appeared. Insects buzzed and a bird screeched—an osprey, it sounded like. Some little bird landed on one of the lounge chairs. "Security cameras or something. Not exactly great TV," Sarah said, clicking on a different date.

There were more video feeds from the pool area and the hallways.

"Oh!" Sarah suddenly looked horrified. "What if there are cameras in our *rooms*!"

"They couldn't do that." I clicked on a few more, then looked around the office. "The cameras aren't hidden or anything. Look. . . ." I pointed to one in the corner. And then I froze. "That means it's recording us right now."

Sarah held her breath for a second, then waved her hand at the camera. "Nah, we're fine. We have security cameras at my school, but my friend Claire's dad is the principal, and he says no one ever looks at the video unless there's a theft or vandalism or something."

That made sense. I took a deep breath and clicked open another video file. This one was of Ben on a treadmill, Dr. Ames at his side like a coach. "He's started exercise therapy already? I thought Dr. Ames said we had to wait a few days for Phase Two."

I felt a twinge of jealousy. I was following all their rules; how come Ben was getting faster treatment?

Sarah shrugged. "They must think he's ready. His chart thing said low risk. Let's look at this one." She moved the cursor to the Subjects folder. Inside were two subfolders: Past and Current. Inside the Past folder were dozens of files—probably more than a hundred—arranged in alphabetical order. Sarah opened the first one. It was full of MRI images and data for someone named Jenna Aberdeen, whose last scan was dated four months ago.

"She must have been a patient," Sarah said.

"Who got better. And went home. Sarah, maybe we're over-reacting. Maybe—"

"Look at this one." She clicked the Current file; it held only six folders: Enriquez, Grayson, Hayes, Jacobs, McCain, and Perkins. Sarah clicked on hers.

"It's the same as the one in the hallway," I said. "Can we go now?" My headache was coming back, and every time I thought about Dr. Ames or Dr. Gunther walking in on us, I felt nauseous.

"Five minutes. I want to read his e-mail." She pointed to Dr. Gunther's mail icon. "I used to read my brother's all the time. I got some great dirt on him until he password-protected it."

Dr. Gunther didn't have a password. His in-box opened right up.

Subject	Sender	Date
April Newsletter	Amer. Neurological Society	Today 13:45
Re: Interview Request	B. Kenyon	Today 11:48
Re: Data Request	MSON	Today 11:15
Auction #098742l	eBay Seller morphoman	Today 10:55
Re: Lab Preparations	Andrei Hausen	Today 06:33

GoogleAlert: Al Jihada	Google Alerts	Monday 23:29
FW: Moscow 5/7	Mark Ames	Monday 23:10
Auction #098742	eBay Seller morphoman	Monday 22:55
Re: Moscow 5/7	Mark Ames	Monday 18:10
GoogleAlert: Al Jihada	Google Alerts	Monday 12:49
Interview Request	B. Kenyon	Monday 12:08
Re: Schaus Swallowtail	eBay Seller morphoman	Monday 10:55
Team Phoenix	R. J. Wiley	Monday 10:49
Re: Schaus Swallowtail	eBay Seller morphoman	Monday 09:11
GoogleAlert: Al Jihada	Google Alerts	Monday 07:09

I sank down in a chair as Sarah skimmed the e-mail. "There's a bunch of news alerts on some terrorist group."

"Why would he get alerts on that?"

Sarah shrugged. "Maybe he's paranoid terrorists will attack the clinic."

"Out here in the middle of nowhere?" I sighed. "Maybe back when it was a military base, but not now."

"Hmm . . ." Sarah scrolled down. "There's a neurology society newsletter, some Team Phoenix thing—maybe he's in a fantasy football league. My brother does that. There's a note from Andrei somebody about lab preparations . . . another one from some reporter who wants to do an interview about poachers in the area."

"Molly talked about that," I said.

". . . and he bought something on eBay." Sarah went on. She clicked the mouse. "A butterfly, for . . . four hundred and twenty-eight dollars? It's not even that pretty."

I stood up to look.

The butterfly in the image wasn't as striking as the blue morpho or Queen Alexandra's Birdwing on Dr. Gunther's wall. This one was mostly black-brown, with some pale-yellow markings and a few touches of orange and blue near its tail.

"What about that one?" I pointed to another e-mail.

"It's from Dr. Ames . . . about plane tickets. Looks like they're taking a trip to Moscow next month."

I felt like my brain had some kind of switch flipping back and forth.

Everything's fine.

No, it's not.

Everything's fine.

Something's not right.

"Moscow?" *Something's not right.*

Sarah scrolled through the e-mail. "Yeah. I wonder who's going to be here with us. Substitute doctors? I hope they're not leaving us with Olga. She's always grumpy."

"Maybe we'll be home by then."

"None of this is very interesting." Sarah closed the e-mail program.

"What's this folder?" I pointed to the corner of the screen, to the folder labeled Research. The word made me think about experiments. Last spring, Lucy's mom had taken us on a tour of the lab where she works at Stanford. There were rows and rows of cages along one wall, most full of white mice and rats, but a few rabbits, too.

"Those are our research animals," she'd told us. "They're used to test medicines so we can make sure they're safe for people."

I remembered feeling awful for the rabbits in those little cages.

Research.

What kind of research was Dr. Ames doing?

I clicked on the folder, but there were no mice or rats or rabbits inside—just more folders labeled with names.

Curie

Da Vinci

Edison

Einstein

Gunther

Meitner

Newton

Oppenheimer

Shilling

"I don't recognize all of them, but some of these names are scientists and inventors," I said. "Da Vinci . . . Einstein . . . Edison . . ."

"Gunther?" Sarah raised her eyebrows.

"Yeah . . . he's not exactly in the same league."

"Maybe *he* thinks he's famous," Sarah said.

She clicked on the Edison folder. Inside were a dozen or so files—Early Life, Education, Phonograph, Electric Light, Laboratory Notes, Menlo Park, Fort Myers Estate, Botanical Research, Relationship with Ford. "This looks like stuff you'd collect for a research paper. Why would Dr. Gunther need it? He hasn't been in school for, like, a million years."

"Some weird hobby?" I guessed. "Like his thing with butterflies?" The switch in my head flipped. *Everything's fine.* My headache was getting worse; I wanted to sleep. "If you want to stay, you can, but I'm going to my room."

"Come on, Cat. Those MRIs take forever. We have time." And she went back to the video files.

"I'm leaving." I headed for the door, but a deep voice that came from the computer stopped me.

"No! Not when we're so close!"

I shivered, even though the room was warm. I'd overheard those words hours ago; now I turned to the screen and saw the fierce look on Dr. Ames's face that went with them.

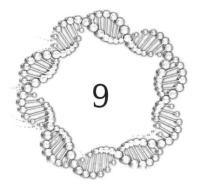

9

"LET IT PLAY." I RUSHED back to Sarah's side. "This is what I heard earlier, standing outside the office."

Dr. Gunther stood next to Dr. Ames in the video, at the same desk Sarah and I hovered over now.

Dr. Gunther was pointing down at images in a manila folder. "It's clear Kaylee Enriquez's tumor is growing. We have to contact her parents, Mark. We can't justify—"

"I said no!"

I looked at Sarah. Her eyes were huge as she stared at the video.

Dr. Gunther put a hand to his temple and rubbed in small circles. "I can't," he said, then mumbled something. I turned the video feed up louder to hear. "This has gone far enough. Think what could happen."

Dr. Ames put both hands flat on the desk then and leaned across, so far that Dr. Gunther pulled away and sank back in his leather chair. I would have done that, too.

"*You* think what could happen, Rudolph. Have you forgotten how we came to work together?"

Now I remembered. Dr. Ames had threatened Dr. Gunther while I was standing outside his door.

"At that time, you were found to be violating federal laws that regulate genetic engineering research. At that time, you were charged with a felony. And at *that* time you were never going to set foot in a lab again. You were never going to finish your clinical research; you were never going to find your cure for Parkinson's disease. And you. Were. Going. To. *Die*."

"Die? From what? That disease?" Sarah whispered.

I put my hands up—*no idea*—and pointed to the video.

"We gave everything back to you, Rudolph. We kept you out of jail. We kept you in the lab. We provided everything you needed for your research. We kept you alive. We kept our part of the deal, and you need to keep yours."

On the video, Dr. Gunther reached for a file on the desk. His hands shook, and he looked up at Dr. Ames. "How much longer?"

"Not long. We're close. And things look much better with the other first-round subject, yes?"

"Perkins. Trent Perkins."

"The procedure has taken?" Dr. Ames tapped his fingers together.

"It seems so, yes. It's early. Too early for cognitive tests to confirm, but we're already seeing personality changes that would indicate success."

"I knew it!" Sarah couldn't stand still any longer. She swiped tears from her eyes and whirled around to face me. "They're *changing* him! They're going to—"

"Shhhh!" I whispered. "We need to hear the rest."

Sarah's face was red, but she took a deep breath and nodded. I started the video again, in time to see Dr. Gunther take a long, shaky breath, too. "Very well. We'll proceed as planned," he said. "But we must contact the girl's parents. The rate of tumor growth is too dramatic to be contained. She'll need surgery, and—"

"No."

"Mark, the child is going to die if we don't—"

"Not yet."

"When?" Dr. Gunther's hand shook as he wiped his brow.

"When our work is done." Dr. Ames leaned over the desk again. "And not a moment before."

"Lord, have mercy. All right." Dr. Gunther nodded and closed his eyes. Dr. Ames stalked out of the room.

Sarah stared at the screen. Dr. Gunther wasn't talking or even moving, but she kept staring as if she could see through to his thoughts.

"Sarah, we have to go," I said finally. There was so much to say, but I didn't know where to start. There was no denying it now, no hoping I was confused. Something was wrong. I knew what I heard, and I was struggling to hang on to the words, even as my headache threatened to swallow them up. I needed to get back to my room, lie down, and think. Or write all this down before it slipped away. "We have to go," I said again.

But Sarah was leaning into the computer, eyes scanning the desktop. "There must be more here."

"It's been too long. We *can't* get caught."

She took a deep breath and bit her lip for a second. "Okay." Sarah followed me away from the desk, but halfway to the door, she wheeled around and rushed back to the computer. "Wait! One more. There was this other file. . . ."

I was so dizzy I gave up and sat down in the chair next to her.

"'DNA Analysis.'" She read the folder's name, then opened it, and the same list of scientist and inventor names came up as file names. Sarah clicked on the one labeled Edison, and a river of random letters poured onto the screen.

"'C-C-G-C-A-G-T'?" Sarah frowned. "It's a bunch of gibberish."

"No." I stared at the screen, willing the letters to come into focus. It wasn't gibberish. I took a couple deep breaths and tried to push the pain back in my head. It worked a little, and I could think again. I knew what those letters were.

"My friend's mom showed me something like this in the lab where she works," I said. "That sequence of letters stands for someone's DNA—their genetic makeup, like, who they are."

"So this is . . . ?"

"This is . . ." My mind formed the words, but they didn't make sense. DNA codes from dead scientists? *Something's not right.* "This is Thomas Edison. I guess."

"Hasn't he been dead a while?"

"Yeah. But . . ." I scrolled through the letters. Was it possible? "DNA lasts a long time after you die. We read an article about it in school. Scientists have gotten DNA from Neanderthal fossils that are seventy thousand years old. That's kind of extreme—but it's totally possible to get some DNA from a person more than a hundred years after they die. The article said they identified the Romanov royal family from the Russian Revolution that way."

Sarah opened the document about Edison's inventions in front of the DNA file, but the letters still filled the screen behind it. "Look at the pictures of this guy." She scrolled through images of a young Edison in his lab, working with plants, sitting at a long table surrounded by gadgets and wires and with a look of fierce concentration from his face. "Geez, he reminds me of Trent at breakfast."

Edison had a cot set up in his laboratory, the text said, so he wouldn't have to leave the lab to sleep. I stared at the picture on the screen. DNA sequences swam behind it.

And Dr. Ames's voice on the roof came back to me more clearly. This time, I was sure of the words I'd heard him say.

. . . by Monday, we'll have four more subjects undergoing the change.

"The change." I whispered the words to myself, trying to make them make sense.

"What?" Sarah asked.

"The change . . . they keep using that phrase. . . . The change. What's the change?"

"Trent sure changed."

She was right. The kid from breakfast was more like the inventor on the screen than the boy Sarah had described.

"Hello?"

We never heard footsteps, but Dr. Ames's voice was close—right down the hall.

"Oh, hey," he went on. "Just finished doing an MRI on Quentin Hayes."

I held a finger to my lips and pointed under the desk. My

hands shook, but I closed the files on Gunther's computer, and we scrambled under the desk, huddled in the shadows. I could feel Sarah next to me, breathing, trying to stay quiet. She smelled like chlorine and suntan lotion.

"Yeah, okay. I'm going to review the scans now."

Go to your own office, I thought. *Down the hall. Not this one.* A searing pain shot through my head, behind my eyes. Stress always made the headaches worse, so bad that I'd vomit sometimes. I couldn't help it. My stomach clenched and I squeezed my knees tight into the cramp. *Not now. Not now.*

"Everything looks fine. He's a perfect candidate, I can already tell. We're in great shape. Hold on a sec, okay?"

His voice was right outside.

Keys jingled. Acid rose in my throat. I clenched my teeth together and swallowed it back down.

Finally, we heard the door down the hall open and slam shut.

We kept waiting. After a minute, maybe two, I unfolded my legs and started to crawl out into the light. "We need to get out of here," I whispered. "Now."

Sarah nodded; her eyes were huge. She didn't look excited to be playing girl detective anymore.

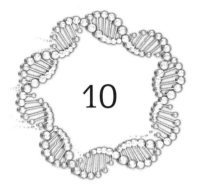

10

"WE NEED TO TALK TO Trent," Sarah insisted. But he was nowhere to be found. We knocked on his room door, checked the labs, the cafeteria . . . everywhere. "He's probably holed up in that workshop or whatever, doing those engineering projects he supposedly loves so much."

We found Quentin and Ben at the pool and told them everything. About the videos and subject folders and DNA stuff we'd found on Dr. Gunther's computer. I told them what I heard Dr. Ames say about "the change."

"Are you suggesting"—Ben put down his magazine—"that these guys who have been running this successful clinic for— what did it say in the brochure, five years?—have actually been doing some kind of evil scientists' experiments the whole time? And nobody's ever noticed until now?" He raised his eyebrows. "You two must be geniuses."

Quentin picked up his towel and dried his face. "I get why you're freaked out by that stuff on the computer—and it *is* freaky—but you *must* be missing something." He shook his head at Sarah. "What you're suggesting . . . They could never get away with that. Wouldn't all the parents have noticed?"

There went the switch in my head again. Saying it out loud, telling the boys about it, made it sound far-fetched. "I don't know. I guess . . ."

"Well maybe the place *used* to be a perfectly normal clinic," Sarah blurted out, "and all the mysterious stuff is . . . new."

"Maybe Dr. Ames is an alien, too!" Ben snorted.

"Sarah, really . . . there has to be an explanation," Quentin said.

"Maybe . . ." The switch in my head flickered. . . .

Everything's okay.

Something's not right.

I hesitated. "Still . . . it wouldn't hurt to try and learn a little more, would it? Maybe we could get phone numbers for some of those kids who were already released and see what they have to say."

"We have to get more information," Sarah agreed. "What about Kaylee? They said she had some tumor or something, and they're not even telling her parents!"

Quentin turned to me. "Are you sure that's what they said?"

"Yes." But then I questioned myself. What were the words, exactly? *If she dies here . . . tumor . . . not yet . . .* "I . . . I think so, anyway."

"It *was*!" Sarah was almost shouting.

"Okay . . . okay." Quentin sighed. "We'll find out more. We can all keep our eyes open. We can talk to Trent whenever he turns up." He looked toward the clinic windows. "You know, we could *ask* Dr. Gunther about those files that—"

"No!" Sarah lowered her voice. "Then he'll know we were snooping and we'll never find anything else. We need to find Trent."

But Trent wasn't at dinner that night. Or at any meals the next day.

The more time that went by, the more I forgot the details of what Sarah and I had seen in the lab. I struggled to hold on to what I knew, or thought I knew. But there was nothing we could do until we found Trent, so I rested in my room a lot. I read and made a clay shape that looked almost like a snail kite I'd seen perched on a pillar by the docks. I took my medicine and showed up for my MRIs. No matter what was going on, I still had to focus on getting better if I wanted to go home.

Finally, as I was finishing my oatmeal at breakfast, Dr. Ames bounded into the room with his clipboard. "Good morning, team! Cat, I've got some great news for you. We're moving you ahead to Phase Two of treatment today. You'll start light and oxygen treatments right after breakfast, and we'll get you on the treadmill later if you're up to it."

"Great!" I said. I meant it, too. If Phase Two could get rid of the rest of my headaches and clear the muddled mess in my brain, I was ready to go. Plus, if Trent was spending more time in the lab during Phase Three, maybe I'd get to talk with him, too.

But when I got to the lab, only Dr. Ames and Olga were there, waiting for me with some weird hat. It looked like my grandma's shower cap, but with tiny lights attached on the inside.

"Ready for your first light treatment?" Dr. Ames said, motioning for me to lie down on the exam table. He stretched out the elastic cap so it fit over my head. It tugged at my hair when he let go. "This helps keep the LED lights in place over your scalp and forehead," he said. "They'll be providing short-term exposure to red and near-infrared rays to facilitate more efficient cell metabolism."

"What does that mean in English?"

"Sorry." He flashed that sheepish grin. "You're getting a good dose of light energy to help your brain cells heal themselves."

"Well, that sounds good." I leaned back and closed my eyes. Ten minutes went by fast, because the next thing I knew, Olga was helping me get the cap off, and Dr. Ames was across the lab, opening up this box that looked like a big glass casket.

"Come on over, Cat, and let's get right to the oxygen treatment so you have some time to relax before lunch."

"How long does this last?" I looked around. Sarah was walking in for her light treatment. She gave me a wave, and I saw her eyes scan the lab, probably looking for Trent.

"You'll be in the chamber for one hour a day, five days a week." He opened the coffin-thing. "Try to relax."

"If they want people to relax in this thing, they should have thought twice about shaping it like a coffin, don't you think?" But I climbed in, and it wasn't too bad. The bottom was padded, so it felt like a cot with a lid.

Dr. Ames put a hand on the glass cover, ready to slide it over the top of me. "You remember what this is all about?"

"Kind of."

"It's the same treatment deep-sea divers get when they're

having decompression sickness," Dr. Ames said. "When I close the lid, you'll be breathing one hundred percent oxygen with a little extra atmospheric pressure, which helps the oxygen dissolve in your blood more quickly so it can flow through your body and help repair those damaged brain cells. Make sense?"

"I guess so." He closed the lid over me. I wondered if he'd still be able to hear me talking. "It feels like I'm in a giant test tube," I said, and Dr. Ames laughed and gave me a thumbs-up. He could hear fine.

I tried to relax and breathe. At first, being in the oxygen chamber felt like taking off in an airplane, and my ears felt weird from the pressure. But then it felt normal, and Dr. Ames turned on music.

Watching through the glass, I saw Sarah leave for the exercise room and Quentin and Ben come in for their light treatments. But never Trent.

And that quiet time all alone in the glass casket gave me too much time to think. Was Trent getting treatments somewhere else? Maybe Phase Three required some different kind of lab, with different equipment. I kept telling myself that, but part of me never believed it. That part was pretty sure the doctors were hiding Trent from the rest of us.

"Where could he *be*?" Sarah asked after our morning treatments. She held open the cafeteria door, followed me inside, looked around, and sighed. "He's not even coming for meals anymore."

She ate her chicken salad sandwich with her eyes on the door. But Trent never showed up.

After lunch, I had my first session on the treadmill. Olga got me hooked up with stuff to monitor my heart rate and blood pressure, and then Dr. Ames arrived.

"Ready to run a marathon?" His eyes crinkled when he smiled. It was hard to imagine this was the same man who yelled at Dr. Gunther on that video. I still couldn't help wondering if there was something we hadn't seen . . . something that happened before the video started that might explain everything.

"I'll do my best." I stepped onto the treadmill, and Dr. Ames started it moving, slowly at first.

"Okay if we try a little faster?" he asked, and when I nodded, he turned it up so it was a good, fast walk.

"Am I going to run?" I'd changed into sneakers just in case, but I was worried it would make me dizzy. I hated that feeling . . . the spinning and blurring, the stomach churning.

"Not today. But I'm going to turn up the incline to get your heart rate up a little. It'll be like walking up a hill."

It felt like I'd been walking uphill for an hour—really it was only about ten minutes—when Dr. Ames looked at the monitors and asked, "How are you doing?"

"Not great," I admitted, and he slowed the machine down. "I'm a little dizzy. And my head is starting to hurt."

"Fair enough," he said, making the incline flat again. "We can call it a day. Tomorrow, you'll push a little more."

Dr. Ames came to get me after breakfast every day for the rest of the week.

It was always just Sarah and Quentin and Ben and me in the

dining room. Never Trent, and never Kaylee, and somehow, the whole *something's-wrong* feeling kind of faded away.

Concussions had a way of doing that . . . dulling memories that seemed big and important once, until they were so blurry you figured they couldn't matter much at all. Even Sarah stopped turning around when the cafeteria door opened. It was always Dr. Ames or Dr. Gunther or Olga anyway.

On Friday, it was Dr. Ames, and as he walked me to the lab, we talked about soccer—he'd never liked it much either, even though he was a starting goalie in high school—and what it's like being an only child. He'd never really wished for siblings, but I thought it would be cool to have a younger sister.

"Yeah, but she'd borrow your clothes and shoes all the time," he joked, helping me with the light therapy cap.

"I doubt that." I held up one foot and wiggled my mud-stained sneaker. "Not if she had any style." It felt good to joke, good to laugh without my head hurting.

I had to admit Phase Two was living up to the promises on the I-CAN website. I felt more like my old self. I'd been swimming a few times. I'd even started reading that magic bread-box book for English class, and I understood now why Mrs. Rock liked it so much. The main character felt real, like she might be your friend or sit next to you in math class, and the fact that she could wish for stuff and then find it in that bread box was fun to think about.

I'd been working on my birds, too. I'd started sculpting a heron, even though its long neck was going to be tricky. The snail kite was finished except for firing and painting, and that would have to wait until I got home.

I couldn't wait to get home. Every time I felt like slowing down on the treadmill, I thought about Mom and Dad, about our houseboat and the bay, and I pushed myself to keep going. I was up to a mile now, and my head only hurt a little at the end.

"Absolutely fantastic!" Dr. Ames high-fived me as I stepped off the treadmill. "You're scheduled for an MRI now, and then you can head outside. But I can already tell you've had a great first week of Phase Two. Really good work, kiddo. We'll be moving on to Phase Three in no time."

"Thanks," I said, but when he mentioned Phase Three, I remembered Trent, and questions tugged at my insides. After spending most of the day with Dr. Ames, it felt safe to ask now. "Do you known where Trent's been lately? We haven't seen him around. Dr. Gunther mentioned some workshop?"

"Oh!" Dr. Ames's eyes looked startled, but only for a second. Then his face relaxed into its usual smile. "Trent was discharged on Wednesday. He's gone home."

"He has?"

"Yep, his foster parents came to pick him up. You must have missed him." Dr. Ames headed for the hallway.

I followed him. "So . . . Trent's all better?"

"Good as new." Dr. Ames held open the lab door. Relief seeped through me like hot chocolate on a cold, rainy day. Quentin was right. Sarah and I had misunderstood all that computer stuff somehow. Trent was fine. He'd gone home, and now that I was getting better, I'd get to go home soon, too. But something still flickered inside me.

I paused. "Can you tell me once more how Phase Three of this treatment works?"

"Sure." Dr. Ames put a hand on my back and gave me a little push to keep me moving through the door, down the hall. "You already know Phase One was simply about getting you settled, getting your meds at the right levels." He stopped at the door to the MRI room and held it open for me. "Phase Two is what you're doing now—the light and oxygen therapies, combined with exercise to help your brain cells repair themselves as much as possible." He clicked a wall switch, and the laboratory lights flickered on. "And Phase Three is the gene therapy. Remember how I explained it when your mom was here?"

"I think so."

"We use retroviruses . . . which get inside cells and use them to replicate their own DNA." He patted the MRI table, and I stretched out on it. "When a retrovirus has healthy human DNA, it can—"

"Healthy human DNA from *where*?" I blurted.

"Remember when your doctor at home took blood for testing?"

I nodded.

"As soon as he referred you to us, he sent that blood sample here. We've been growing *your* DNA, and that's what we use. It works beautifully." He grinned and flipped a switch on the wall, and my table started moving toward the scanner. "Hold still now, okay?"

I held still, but the whole time I was being moved toward that electrical donut that would scan my brain, I couldn't help wondering what had happened to Trent's brain. Did he really used to be that goofy kid Sarah told me all about? If he was, what changed him into the quiet boy-genius we'd seen that one morning at breakfast?

Could that happen if the doctors were using Trent's *own* DNA to repair his damaged brain tissue?

When the MRI table finally slid back out of the donut, Dr. Ames said, "All set, Cat. You can head out for some fresh air unless you have more questions for me."

I did have more questions. But I wasn't ready to ask them yet, so I smiled and went outside. There was a great blue heron flying over. I recognized it right away and wondered if I'd be able to do that once my Phase Three was complete. Would I still know a heron from its pointed toes in flight? Would I be able to shape its long neck out of clay and etch the feathers on its wings? Would I still care?

What was going to happen to me when those new brain cells started to grow?

11

"SEE THAT STRANGLER FIG?" QUENTIN reached into a box for a handful of cereal and then pointed to a tree opposite the dock. Another thinner tree was wrapped around it, over and over, like a python. "It's the smaller one—wrapped around the cypress."

"Yeah." Sarah tossed a Cheerio to the gulls that had gathered around us. "It looks like it's hugging that other tree to death."

I had to laugh. "That's how I felt when Dad hugged me at the airport before I came here." For the first time since I got to I-CAN, I was feeling well enough to enjoy a memory from home with a smile instead of watery eyes. It was amazing what sleeping all night and waking up without a headache could do.

"The tree *is* being hugged to death, literally." Quentin threw a shower of cereal up in the air, and the birds all rose up from the water to squawk over who got what. "The strangler fig is a parasite; it's stealing nutrients from the cypress, and eventually it'll kill its host plant. A virus kind of works that way, too, except it gets *inside* the cells of its host and hijacks them to make copies of itself. It uses your cells to make copies of its own DNA. We studied this in advanced bio. It's what happens when you catch a cold or the flu or something."

Quentin was trying to explain retroviruses to the rest of us, and he was doing a better job than Dr. Ames had. I was finally starting to get it. "So if you somehow change the DNA in that virus . . ." I thought for a second. "Then the virus won't be making copies of itself anymore. It'll be making . . ."

"Whatever you choose." Quentin reached for more cereal. "All you have to do is genetically engineer the virus, so the DNA that it's copying is the kind of DNA you actually *want*. They've been using this kind of gene therapy for a while, to treat some diseases."

"Sounds pretty awesome," Ben said. "Why question it when Trent's better and has already gone home?"

"That's what they *say* happened." Sarah leaned over and held out a piece of cereal to a wary seagull; it came close but wouldn't take it from her. "But the last time we saw Trent, he was a totally different person. And they had all that other DNA data in their files. What if the genetic material they introduced wasn't Trent's? What if they gave him DNA from somebody else?"

"Like . . . oh . . . I don't know . . . a dead scientist?" Ben threw a Cheerio so hard he pegged a duck in the head with it. "Whoops! Thought it was Trent's DNA but maybe it's Albert Einstein's . . . oh well."

"I'm *serious*! I know what we saw." Sarah whipped around to face me. "And so do you. I think you're *trying* to forget."

"I am not." I felt as if she'd slapped me. I wasn't trying to forget. I wasn't . . . but sometimes, when I remembered, it was overwhelming. I was feeling so much better, and the idea that our miracle clinic might not completely fix me after all this was too much to think about. "I just . . . I don't know anymore. But I do know that I'm not dizzy today, and my head doesn't hurt, and that's all I wanted in the first place."

"You know what I want? I want to leave. *Now.* You guys, they're starting Phase Three with Quentin and Ben and me *this* week!"

"Perfect." Ben pretended to check his watch. "Maybe I'll be home for Sunday dinner."

Sarah knocked Ben's plastic cup out of his hand and a shower of little round O's rained into the water. The birds went crazy scarfing them up. "Something is *wrong*, and I don't know what, and yeah, maybe it sounds dumb, but I'm scared."

Ben shrugged.

The only sound was duck bills, opening and closing in the water.

And as soon as I forced myself to think about it again, my head got all fuzzy. But I made myself remember. There *were* too many questions.

What if Sarah was right? The idea of Dr. Ames and Dr. Gunther injecting somebody *else*'s DNA into me was . . . My stomach clenched, and I closed my eyes. "I'm scared, too," I whispered. My eyes burned with hot tears, and the shadow of a headache hung over me. I hated that it was back when I was supposed to be getting better. I couldn't think about it anymore right now. Not until we knew for sure. "We have to find out more."

I thought Quentin and Ben would laugh like they'd been laughing at Sarah all along, but they didn't. Ben only shook his head.

"Can we get back into that office, you think?" Quentin asked. He looked up at the clinic. "Or maybe . . . I think Gunther and Ames are both inside. Scans are done for today. We could try to talk to one of them."

Sarah and I spoke at the same time. "No."

"If we talk about any of this, they'll know we were in the office," Sarah said.

"And I don't trust them." I hadn't realized that until I said it. But I didn't.

"Do you trust anybody?" Quentin asked.

The Cheerios were all gone, and the ducks had paddled away except for one, waiting to see if we'd drop more. There was a single tiny O left on the dock; I brushed it into the water and thought about Lucy. A few months ago, I would have answered his question with her name in a second, but things had changed so much.

A duck came close to snarf up that last piece of cereal, and the fine lines of feathers on its head reminded me of the bird I made for Lucy's birthday. It was a chickadee, and I brought it to her party, all wrapped up in tissue paper in a purple gift bag. When Lucy opened it, she said, "Oh wow! Did you make this?" I nodded and she smiled and set it down on the table next to a stack of iTunes gift cards and a huge jar of pastel M&M'S. I told her it was kind of fragile, but I don't know if she heard, because she was already opening something else, and somehow, my bird got buried in all the bows and torn-open envelopes, and when I was getting cake, I found it on the edge of the table with its beak broken off. I don't know if somebody dropped it or what, but I found the beak under the table. I slipped it into my jacket pocket with the bird when I left to go home. I was planning to fix it and give it back to Lucy at school, but I couldn't make it look right glued back together, so I never did. Lucy never asked about it.

I couldn't say I trusted Lucy anymore. And I didn't have many other friends. I thought about Amberlee from my art class. She'd asked about my birds and invited me to come to art club and might have been a friend if I'd let her. But Lucy and Corinne were in charge of our cafeteria table, and they'd said no, and I hadn't said anything at all.

"Cat?" Sarah's voice brought me back. I kind of trusted Sarah, but I hardly knew her. Who was left?

I took a deep breath. "I trust my parents and Aunt Beth and Kathleen." I folded my arms over my chest. It was weird, but then I thought about Sawgrass Molly, her dark eyes and her weathered hands and all she knew about this place. "And Molly. Maybe we should talk to Molly."

"Her boat's here." Sarah nodded toward the airboat, tied up to the dock. "I haven't seen her, though. She wasn't up at the clinic."

Quentin looked around. "She's not out on the grounds. But what's in there?" He pointed toward the older building we'd seen on the property the day we arrived.

"Old storage building, I think Dr. Ames said. It's probably from when this was a military property." I stood up, brushed the cereal crumbs from my lap, and took a deep breath. "Maybe it's a garage or something. Molly could be up there. Let's go see."

"Fine." Ben rolled his eyes, but I didn't care. We needed to find Molly. We needed someone who could tell us we were going to be okay.

"Looks pretty abandoned," Sarah said as we got closer. The building was a rust-covered shell that must have been important once but didn't look like it mattered to anyone besides barn swallows anymore. "I bet it's locked."

Faded green paint peeled off the door, but when Quentin reached for the handle, it turned, and we stepped into an echoey cave of a room. It was gigantic, mostly empty except for an old silver-and-red plane in the far corner. There was a number on the tail and U.S. AIR FORCE painted on the side.

"That plane's gotta be from the fifties or sixties!" Quentin jogged over to it and ran his hand along the wing. "Somebody's taken it apart. The engine's gone." He hoisted himself up to peer into the cockpit. "All the navigation stuff's torn up, too."

He jumped down, and his sneakers thudded on the cement floor. "I don't think Molly's—"

Something clanged—metal on metal—from another part of the hangar, and we all turned. Tucked behind the plane was the entrance to a hallway that ran along one wall of the building. Quentin started down it, but I grabbed his sleeve. "What if it's not Molly? What if it's Dr. Ames? Or Dr. Gunther?"

"So what?" Quentin said. "Nobody said we couldn't come in here."

"True." But it still felt dangerous. "Let's go. Just be careful."

The clanging got louder as we crept down the hall. Sarah walked so close behind me she kept stepping on the backs of my sneakers.

At the end of the hallway was a single door with a tiny rectangular window. The clanging was coming from right inside, over and over. Quentin took a deep breath and stepped up to the window.

His mouth fell open.

"What?" I whispered. "Is it Dr. Ames? Dr. Gunther?"

He shook his head. "It's Trent."

12

"LOOK AT HIM," QUENTIN WHISPERED, and stepped aside so I could see through the dirty glass.

Trent sat on a high stool, leaning over a long, narrow table filled with engine parts and wires, batteries and radio transmitters, what looked like the old plane's navigational instruments, all strung together, and other electronics I couldn't recognize. It had to be the workshop Dr. Gunther mentioned in the cafeteria. The room was about the size of the swimming pool, with two more tables lined up behind the first one, all overflowing with scientific equipment—beakers and test tubes on one table, nests of tangled wires and gadgets on the others. The walls were floor-to-ceiling shelves filled with more electronics, supplies, and books . . . rows and rows of books. Trent sat in the center of it all, focused with the intensity of the sun.

I tapped on the glass, but he didn't look up. He was lost in the connections in his hands, lost in that other world.

"Dr. Ames lied," I said, still staring. "Trent is *here*."

Sarah put her hand on the doorknob, jiggled it, and shook her head. "Trent!" She hollered and rapped her fist on the glass. Trent didn't even look up. "How could he not hear me?"

I shivered, watching him reach for another mess of wires. "He's turned into some kind of . . ." It still sounded impossible, so I didn't say it out loud. But when I saw the cot in the corner of the room, I knew.

"It looks like Edison's lab in there," Sarah whispered.

I nodded slowly. It was Edison's lab. And right in the middle of it, a boy who used to love playing basketball and goofing around, acting exactly like Thomas Edison.

"They *did* give him someone else's DNA," I said quietly. "They must have. What else could this *be*?" I still couldn't believe it.

Ben never said a word. He stared through the glass, mouth open, eyes confused.

"This is incredible." Quentin squinted through the glass, and I followed his eyes, taking in every corner of the lab. "Someone set up this workshop for Trent, set it up with everything an inventor could possibly want, filled it with a personal library."

His words bounced around my brain and mixed with other words, in another voice.

Phase Three . . . Piece of cake . . . Ask my buddy Trent.

Suddenly, I was afraid of even being here, seeing this. "You guys, we have to go. We can wait for Molly at her boat."

It felt wrong to leave Trent, but we did. He looked happy enough. Did he even know how much he'd changed? If he did, he didn't seem to care.

"I don't understand *how* it could work," Quentin said as we crossed the lawn, heading down to the docks. "When we studied genetics for Science Olympiad, we learned all about cloning and genetic engineering, and what happened here . . . it shouldn't even be *possible*."

"You saw him, Quentin." Sarah ran ahead of him and turned to face him, walking backward. "This is *real*."

"No. This is *stupid*," Ben said. He'd been lagging behind us but caught up. "There's got to be another explanation. Dr. Ames wouldn't *do* something like this."

"Seriously?" Sarah got right in his face, and even though she was a head shorter than he was, Ben took a step back. "You've known Dr. Ames, what, a week? And you're happy to ignore all this because, 'Oh, well, *Dr. Ames* told me everything's great.' Wake up, will you?"

Ben looked as if he might reach out and shove her, but then he actually laughed a little. "You know what? Go have your investigation." He whirled around and stalked off toward the pool.

"This is totally messed up," Quentin said as the rest of us headed for the dock. "I can't imagine how—"

"They *have* Edison's DNA letters . . . or . . . whatever they're called," I said. "We saw the file on Dr. Gunther's computer."

Quentin swatted at a deerfly buzzing around his head. "What else was on that computer?"

"A bunch of random stuff." I tried to remember. "E-mails about a trip Dr. Gunther's taking, one about a team in Phoenix from somebody named Wiley, news alerts about a terrorist group, butterflies he bought on eBay, something from a reporter asking about poachers. Random stuff. But those files . . . the files had DNA sequences."

"But even if you *could* get Edison's DNA to grow inside a living person's cells with retroviruses or whatever, that doesn't mean you'd have a new Edison. Your DNA is only part of what makes you the person you are. People are more than genes. We're this crazy mix of our DNA plus all the experiences we've ever had. All the education, all the people who have been part of our lives, and—"

"They have that, too," I interrupted, remembering the pages and pages of Edison's history, his journals and lab notebooks. "On the computer. They have files full of Edison's past. What if they . . . I don't know . . . gave all that to Trent?"

"How?" Quentin frowned and thought for a minute. "I mean, it sounds totally science fiction, but I guess it would be possible to implant a microchip in his brain so that—"

"That must be it!" Sarah's face was a twisted mix of triumph and fear.

"So they're programming him like a robot?" I shook my head and almost laughed. These were doctors. Hundreds of patients had been treated at this clinic; we'd seen their names on the computer. My mom brought me because it offered the best care in the world for my injury. "That's so crazy. There *has* to be some other explanation." But even as I said it, I remembered Dr. Ames using the word *implant* on the roof. I remembered Trent's bandaged head at breakfast. I tried to push the memories down; I didn't want to think about it, but Sarah grabbed my arm.

"If they did that, Trent would have all those memories *and* Edison's DNA," she said. "He'd have Edison's voice in his head from all those lab notebooks and journals. And then what if they built him that lab and did everything else they could to make him think and work like Edison?"

Quentin paused at the edge of the dock. *"Why?"*

The air cooled as a cloud moved in front of the sun. Sarah didn't have an answer. We stepped onto the dock and walked down to the airboat. Molly still wasn't back, and everything that had been coming together in my head fell apart again. None of this made sense.

"Why would somebody want a dead scientist?" Quentin sat down on the dock and leaned back, looking at the clouds. "Who were the scientists in that file?"

I walked back and forth on the wooden planks. "There was Edison, obviously. And Isaac Newton . . . he discovered gravity, right?"

"More than that," Quentin said. "He made breakthroughs in chemistry and optics and *invented* calculus. My Science Olympiad coach says Newton may have contributed more to science than anybody else in history. Who else?"

I tried to remember the whole list of names from Gunther's computer. "Let's see. There was that Renaissance painter Da Vinci. They had a show on him at the San Francisco Art Museum. There were some women . . . Lise Mitner or Meitner . . . Somebody Shilling . . . Mary Curie . . ."

"*Marie* Curie," Quentin corrected, and let out a low whistle. "Nobel Prize winner in Physics and Chemistry. She basically figured out radioactivity and discovered radium and polonium. She ended up dying of radiation poisoning but not before she accomplished a ton of stuff."

"There might have been one more," I said.

"There was Gunther—but he doesn't count," Sarah called

over from where she was dangling her feet in the water. "And somebody else . . . Redenbacher?"

Quentin tipped his head, confused. "Orville Redenbacher ran a popcorn company."

"No, that's not it," I said. "It was Open-something. Open-hammer?"

"Oppenheimer?" Quentin sat up. "Robert Oppenheimer?"

"Yeah. That's it! Who's he?" Sarah asked.

Quentin ignored her question. "Oppenheimer *and* Curie . . ." He looked up and squinted into the sky for a long time. "You said there was stuff in Gunther's e-mail about a terrorist group?"

"Yeah . . . news alerts."

He stared at the clouds some more. Finally, he shook his head and took a deep breath. "It's kind of nuts . . . but I think I know why someone might want a bunch of dead scientists."

I waited. I wanted everything to make sense before it all fell apart again in my mind, before my headache came back, and I could already feel it pushing behind my eyes.

"What if . . ." Quentin paused. "What if they wanted to bring back all the smartest people from history to . . . work on a project together?"

Sarah tipped her head. "A project?"

I didn't get it either. It sounded like they were going to be some superteam for a school science fair. "Like what kind of project?"

"It could be anything. The right group of scientists might be able to cure cancer or fix global warming or find new energy sources." Quentin thought longer, then let out a sigh. "Or what if they wanted a team to create some . . . super weapon?"

"A super weapon?" I repeated. Hanging in the muggy air, the words sounded silly. For a second, I thought he was kidding.

Sarah did, too. "Are you making fun of me like Ben? Because I don't need this." She got to her feet and started to walk away.

"No. I'm *serious*," Quentin said. "I swear . . . Think about it. If you could bring together all the greatest minds from history, all the greatest thinkers, to work together with modern technology, stuff like Trent's got in there and more," Quentin said. "Imagine what they could create."

"Yeah . . . but . . ." Sarah shook her head, and I understood why.

"But listen," Quentin said. "You said there was something about a terrorist group in Gunther's e-mail. Imagine if you were were part of that group. If you were going after the most powerful nations on earth, you'd need powerful weapons. And you'd need people who could create something bigger, better than ever before."

"But that would mean . . ." I wanted to argue. If he was right, it meant our parents had dropped us off in the middle of nowhere and entrusted us to . . . terrorists? Or at the very least, someone working for terrorists. It sounded like it should be part of a spy movie . . . not my *life*.

It was too much to believe, and thinking about it fueled the headache growing behind my eyes, the headache that was supposed to be gone because I was getting better. "I'm leaving." I stood up and started toward the clinic.

"Cat, wait. Listen . . ."

"No!" I whirled around and shouted back at the dock. "These are *doctors*, Quentin, and they're supposed to be helping us, and this is just . . . no! The idea that somebody's going to mess with a bunch of kids' DNA and turn them into geniuses and then throw them together and say, 'Build me a big new weapon' . . . it's crazy."

Quentin met my yelling with scary quiet. "It's been done before," he said.

"*What?*" Sarah stared at him.

"Not the genetic engineering part. But the idea of bringing geniuses together to build a weapon," Quentin's voice shook. "The Manhattan Project. In the 1940s . . . the United States government assembled a team of scientists in the middle of nowhere to work on a top secret project to defeat Japan during World War Two."

My stomach twisted, and I almost choked on the words, but I blurted them out. "Robert Oppenheimer was one of them, wasn't he?"

Quentin nodded. "They call him the Father of the Atomic Bomb."

13

"YOU KIDS TRYING TO SNEAK off with my airboat?"

We hadn't heard Molly coming down from the clinic, and her booming voice scared me half to death.

"Relax, Cat. I'm just having fun with you. Want to go for a ride and spot some birds?"

"No." My voice quivered. Not because of Molly. But because everything Quentin had said made sense. Frightening, terrifying sense.

"No," I said again. The pieces were coming together in my brain faster and faster, and there was nothing I wanted more than to shake them all back up, unpiece the puzzle, and believe that we were safe here.

But headache or no headache, I couldn't ignore the picture that had formed.

Molly put a hand on my shoulder. "What is it?"

I didn't know where to start.

But Quentin did. He turned and headed for the hangar. "We need to show you something."

Molly stared through the tiny pane of glass, cursing under her breath. She hadn't said a word as we walked, as we told her the whole story, from the conversation on the roof, to the scientist files and DNA sequences, to Dr. Ames, lying about Trent leaving the clinic.

She asked lots of questions:

"Tell me again exactly what Dr. Ames said about Trent going home."

"What else was on that computer?"

"Who was Dr. Gunther e-mailing?"

"Wiley? Do you remember more names?"

And to Sarah: "Trent never expressed an interest in this stuff before?"

We answered all her questions, and she listened, her eyes growing sharper, more concerned with every response. Molly didn't say we were dumb kids or scared about being away from home or anything else. She finished asking questions, and then she looked through that window for a long time, shaking her head, and finally turned to face us.

"We need to get you out of here."

"Can you call for help?" Sarah asked her. "Our cell phones don't work here, so . . ." But Molly was already shaking her head.

"Those e-mails you saw . . . Do you understand the connections here? Do you know who Mark Ames is?"

"He's in charge of the clinic," Quentin said. But that wasn't what she meant.

"Mark Ames is the nephew of R. J. Wiley. United States

Senator Robert Jacob Wiley," she went on. "The most powerful politician in the state of Florida *and* the head of the Senate Armed Services Committee. We need to get you out of here before anyone else finds out about this. If the wrong people find out that you know—"

"Can't you call the police?" Quentin asked, and Molly looked at him as if he had three heads.

"Half the police around these parts are crooked as a gnarled mangrove root." Her eyes darted down the hallway. "Until you're in a safe place, we can't risk—"

"Who's there?" a deep voice called from the main hangar. The echo off the concrete made it sound supernatural. But I knew who it was.

"Dr. Ames!" I whispered.

Molly cursed under her breath and looked around frantically, but we were at the end of a long, windowless hallway, in front of its only door, and that door was locked, with Trent inside.

"Stay here," she hissed. "And don't come out. No matter what. I'll take care of this." She took off running down the hall.

Sarah squeezed my arm, and she clung to Quentin's hand on the other side. We crouched down low along the wall, even though there was no place to hide, and we listened.

"Hello, Mark!" All the fear was gone from Molly's voice. "I'm so glad you're here. I've got a broken fan engine on the airboat. Figured there might be some spare parts around the old hangar."

"Where have you been?"

"I was about to head down the hallway when I heard you. Wasn't there an old storage room around?"

"Who were you talking to?"

My stomach twisted. A dagger of pain shot through my right eye. I squeezed my knees to my chest and tried not to throw up.

But Molly laughed. "Ah, just the mosquitoes and the sky. So many years in the swamp, you get to be pretty good company for yourself."

Dr. Ames said something I couldn't hear. There were footsteps, and finally, the door to the hangar slammed shut.

We waited until we heard the roar of an airboat fan starting, and then we crept down the hall, back into the plane room, and peered out a dusty window.

Both Dr. Ames and Molly were on board, pulling away from the dock on an airboat that quite obviously worked just fine.

14

NOBODY COULD EAT, BUT WE sat in the cafeteria because it was lunchtime, and there was nothing else to do. Dr. Ames was gone with Molly. Dr. Gunther was in the lab with Ben. Both their office doors were closed and locked—Sarah checked. Now she sat turning a turkey sandwich over and over in her hands as if the bread might have answers printed on its crust.

"We need to get back on that computer." Sarah tipped her head. "Do you hear that?" She dropped her sandwich and ran to the half-open window that looked out on the lawn.

We followed her. The dock was still empty except for the kayaks, but the unmistakable hum of an approaching airboat cut through the afternoon haze.

"Molly!" Sarah started for the door.

"Wait." Quentin stepped in front of her. "Dr. Ames probably came back with her. If we go rushing up to the boat and he's on it . . . and he's still angry . . ." Quentin shook his head.

"But we need her," Sarah argued.

We did. But Quentin was right. "She's no good to us if Dr. Ames is still with her." My eyes fell on Sarah's ever-present Frisbee, resting on the table by her sandwich. I'd taken headache medicine at lunch, and it was starting to kick in. I could do this. "Let's play Frisbee."

"*Now?*" Sarah said.

"Perfect." Quentin pointed out the window to the lawn near the dock, and Sarah understood. She grabbed her Frisbee, and we went outside, heading for the lawn as the airboat rounded a bend in the trees.

Sarah stopped. "That's not Molly."

This boat was bigger and older looking, with a tall, stocky man at the control panel. It had fewer seats—most of the deck was open, as if the boat was meant for cargo, not people. The man at the controls killed the engine and tied a rope to a cleat so Dr. Ames could climb onto the dock.

"Where do you think—"

Quentin gave me a light shove and motioned across the grass. He held up the Frisbee and I realized we'd been staring. The strange airboat was already starting up again, its driver easing away from the dock. And Dr. Ames was striding across the lawn.

"Monkey in the middle!" I shouted, jogging in the other direction, and Sarah sent the Frisbee soaring over Quentin's head. I caught it, tossed it back, and snuck a glance toward Dr. Ames. He marched toward the clinic door, clutching a thick Priority Mail package in one hand. His other hand was clenched in a fist.

"Cat! Get it!" Sarah called, but Quentin rushed past me and snagged the Frisbee before I even remembered we were playing.

"You're in the middle," he said, then passed close beside me and whispered, "Did you see that? He's even madder now."

"He had a package. He must have gotten the mail in town," I said, staring up at the clinic. What could have made him so furious?

I backed away from Quentin toward the clinic wall where I thought Dr. Gunther's office must be. The window was open halfway, like always.

"Hey, aren't you in the middle?" Sarah hollered.

"Let's just toss it around, okay? We can make a triangle." I pointed out the shape on the lawn, leaving Sarah where she was, putting Quentin by the sidewalk that led from the clinic to the dock in case Dr. Ames came back, and ending with me . . . right outside the open window.

"Sore loser," Quentin said, but he nodded and jogged over to his spot while I inched toward the window. I didn't want to look sneaky, but I also didn't want to make enough noise that Dr. Gunther might notice and close it. Because if my guess was right . . .

"What in the blazes is wrong with you!" Dr. Ames's voice bellowed out the window over the lawn; we all heard. Dr. Gunther must have answered because then Dr. Ames shouted, "I'll tell you what I'm talking about!"

But he didn't. It was quiet, except for my heart thumping in my ears.

"Catch!" Quentin tossed the Frisbee. It sailed high and to my left. I thought it was a terrible throw until I realized that going to pick it out of the flowers put me right underneath the window.

I bent down to grab the Frisbee, then squatted in the mulch holding my breath. No more words came out the window, but there was a clicking sound. Someone typing on a keyboard, maybe. Typing *hard.*

I glanced at Quentin. He mouthed the words "Can you see?" He made imaginary binoculars out of his hands, then pointed to the window.

I left the Frisbee where it was, put my hands on my knees, and pushed myself to stand on one side of the window. The keyboard sounds had stopped. I held my breath and leaned toward the window, close enough to see the backs of both of their heads. They were facing Dr. Gunther's computer—or Dr. Ames was, anyway. Dr. Gunther leaned on the desk, with his head tipped down, palms covering his face.

Dr. Ames leaned past him and attacked the keyboard again.

"Was there something you wanted to tell me about this? And this?" More fierce keyboard tapping. "And this! Three illegal butterflies in the clinic's PO box in Everglades City, and who's standing by the counter but that reporter, Kendall or Kenyon or whatever his name is. 'Would you have a few minutes to talk with me?' he says. Says he's doing an investigative piece on poaching in the areas bordering the national park. 'You know, gators, butterflies, things like that,' he says. And would I know anything about correspondence between an online dealer who's known to traffic in illegal specimens and someone named Rudolph Gunther?"

Dr. Gunther's hands shook as he reached for the package at the corner of his desk. Dr. Ames knocked it to the floor and whirled around so he was facing both Dr. Gunther and the window.

I dropped down in the flower bed just in time. At least I didn't think he saw me. Bits of bark dug into my knees, but I stayed frozen, my breath catching in my chest. I glanced up at Quentin and Sarah. They were sprawled on the lawn, making whistles of grass blades. But their eyes were locked on me.

More angry words soared over my head, loud enough to be heard across the lawn.

"Do you have any idea—any *idea*—what kind of danger this puts the project in? You and your ridiculous insect fetish. We could be ruined!"

Dr. Gunther's voice was quieter. "I have done everything you've asked me to do, God help me, and it is almost done. Leave my butterflies out of this. I've only ever dealt with reputable sellers, and—"

"They're poachers, for God's sake, Rudolph. Fish and Wildlife is all over them. This asinine reporter is all over them—and now they're after us. And on top of that, I caught Molly snooping around the old hangar. I don't know if she saw him, but either way, I'm going to take care of it. *And* I have a phone message from Kaylee Enriquez's parents."

Dr. Gunther didn't say anything about Kaylee. Or if he did, it was too quiet for me to hear. Then Dr. Ames exploded.

"You called them, didn't you? *Didn't you!*"

"They called me." Dr. Gunther's voice was pleading. "They asked how she was doing. They asked to speak with her, Mark, and she can barely speak. What was I to say?"

"That's it." I heard a loud thump, like a hand slapping wood. "We're moving everything up. Look, R. J. already chartered a private plane, and—"

"For next month." Dr. Gunther sounded like a little kid

trying to answer a teacher's question right. "May seventh, yes? I got the e-mail. It will all be done by—"

"It will be done *now*! We're rescheduling for next week." In that second, Dr. Ames's voice dropped from screaming loud to chillingly calm. "You have until Friday to finish the procedure—complete Phase Three for all four of them—stabilize the subjects, and remove every shred of evidence from this facility before that plane leaves."

I heard footsteps, heard Dr. Gunther's office door open and slam shut. And finally, I rose to my feet and started back to Quentin and Sarah, my hand clutching the Frisbee, my head swimming with words.

Molly snooping . . .

Finish the procedure . . . Complete Phase Three . . .

For all four of them.

By the time I handed Sarah the Frisbee, one thing was clear to me.

"We have to get away from here."

Quentin nodded. "Fast."

15

OUTSIDE SEEMED LIKE THE SAFEST place for us to talk, so
we went back to tossing the Frisbee. Every time I came close to
Sarah and Quentin, I told them more of what I'd heard.

"So what's the deal with the airplane?" Sarah asked.

"I'm not sure." I backed up a little so she could throw the
Frisbee to me. "It sounds like the same thing as the Moscow trip
we read about in Dr. Gunther's e-mail. Now it's next week." I
threw to Quentin, way short so he'd have to come closer.

"We're supposed to be *done* with treatments by next week?"
Sarah's face looked pale.

"By Friday, he said."

Quentin turned the Frisbee over in his hands, thinking. "We
have to get out *before* they start Phase Three. I'll talk to Ben; he'll
come around."

"They could start tomorrow." I thought of Trent, locked up
with his batteries and wires and somebody else's thoughts.

"I know." Quentin nodded, backing up. "So we need to leave

tonight." He threw the Frisbee way over our heads, and when Sarah and I turned to get it, Dr. Gunther was shuffling out the clinic door.

"Have you seen Molly?" He looked even frailer than usual. "I was hoping for a ride into town."

Dr. Ames appeared behind him in the doorway. "Molly's no longer with us," he said briskly. "She quit this afternoon."

"Quit?" I blurted. "Why?"

Dr. Ames tipped his head and looked at me in a way that chilled my insides, but I forced my voice to stay calm. "I mean, I thought she really liked driving that boat."

"I'm sure she does. But she's no longer driving for us." His face relaxed into a smile. "No worries. I've already found a replacement. But he's not available again until tomorrow. Until then, I'm afraid you're stuck with the kayaks if you want to get out and do any bird watching."

"Oh! Well . . . that's okay." I made myself smile, forced myself to meet his eyes, even though they made me want to run. "You can get closer to the birds that way anyway."

After dinner, we walked down to the docks. Sarah wore my binoculars around her neck. We told Dr. Ames I was taking everyone bird watching, and he laughed.

"Your hobby's catching on around here, Cat-Girl."

Ben came, too. Quentin had talked with him, told him everything we heard. I don't know if Ben believed it all, but he came. We'd have to worry about Trent later.

"How are we going to find Molly?" Sarah asked as we untied the kayaks. Blood whooshed in my ears when I bent down, and I had to grab the edge of the dock to steady myself. Quentin and Ben pushed off in the first kayak and waited for us. "Do you know where she lives?"

"No. But I know where she stops to get dinner." I took a deep breath and lowered myself into the boat. When Sarah climbed in behind me, the kayak dipped under her weight, and I winced. But then it steadied, and I took a deep breath and paddled toward the mangrove tunnel. After a few strokes, the rhythm of dipping right, then left, came back to me and calmed my churning stomach.

"It's this way." I led Sarah through the mangroves. It was shady with the sun so low in the sky. Branches stretched above us and cast shadows like thick water snakes under the surface.

Sarah's voice came from behind me. "Where are we going?"

"When Molly brought Ben and me here, she showed us these blue crab traps she sets." My paddle snagged on a mangrove root; we had to backtrack to free it. "She said she checks them around sunset. Maybe she'll be there."

"Maybe." Sarah didn't sound convinced, and her voice sucked the hope out of me. I'd been holding on to the idea— *maybe she'll be there*—but it seemed unlikely now.

When we came out of the mangroves, the sky was tinged yellow-pink. Quentin and Ben were waiting in the clearing.

"It's this way." I pointed to the left. Ahead of us, a mangrove island grew, thick and green, wild limbs reclaiming what must have been a small camp, pulling its boards apart, down into the mud. Soon, the whole thing would be part of the swamp again.

"Wasn't that big alligator around here?" Ben asked, holding

his paddle above the water, drifting. My eyes searched the shadows along the shoreline. I didn't see the gator, but a little green heron fluttered up out of the reeds, wings splashing.

"There!" Sarah pointed up ahead on our right, where One-Eyed Lou guarded a messy nest of sticks and grass. Three yellow-and-black-striped babies rested on her back.

"Give her plenty of room." I paddled hard on the right so the kayak turned left, and we swung a wide circle around Lou and her babies. She watched us through heavy-lidded eyes, her thick front legs spread over the nest, clutching the sides.

"Molly's crab traps were up here on the right, I think." I was pretty sure, but it was so easy to get disoriented, to lose track of all the turns of the grassy river's bends, which side of which dotted island we were on.

We paddled close to the shore, ducking under tree limbs, and spiderwebs brushed my face and arms. "Here's one." I remembered the mangrove tree; its roots splayed out into the water like umbrella spokes in a perfect dome. The metal-caged trap rested on the shallow bottom nearby.

"Has she been here already?" Quentin asked, leaning over to peer into the water.

"I don't think so." I could make out ghostly white crab shapes in the trap and a flash of blue when one turned a fat claw.

"Okay." Sarah dipped the end of her paddle in the water, pulled it out, dipped it in again. "So we just . . . wait?"

"I'm not going to sit here all night." Ben slapped a mosquito on his arm. It left a splotch of blood. "Let's paddle around and see if we find her."

Ben started pushing forward, but Quentin stuck his paddle in the water, and their kayak slowed. "We can't go far," Quentin said. "Maybe around this curve, but after that, the river branches all over the place. We don't have a map or GPS or anything."

"What's that?" Ben pointed through the trees at a flash of light ahead. Late-afternoon sun reflected off something metallic.

We paddled around the bend and found Sawgrass Molly's airboat tied up to the trees.

"See!" Ben said. Molly was nowhere to be found, but there was a hint of a trail leading through the brush.

I pointed it out. "Maybe she's at one of those old camps."

We paddled the kayaks to the edge of the mangroves. Oozy mud sucked at my sneakers when I climbed out.

"Come on." Quentin offered Ben his hand. Ben ignored it and almost fell in the water, but he caught a branch and started up the trail. It didn't go far before the brush filled in, and we were climbing over snapping branches and mangrove roots thick as my arm.

"Did you hear that?" Sarah grabbed my arm. We stopped and listened.

It was quiet.

I looked at Quentin. His eyes narrowed, and I could tell he was thinking what I was thinking.

It was *too* quiet for the Everglades.

A minute earlier, we'd been paddling through the steady whine of millions of tiny insects, the buzz-saw hum of cicadas, the peeping and chirping of frogs, the looping call of a whip-poor-will, over and over and over.

Now there was nothing.

Except . . . "That!" Sarah whispered. "Did you hear that?"

There was a rustle, the crack of a branch. It was close.

We could have run, but we wouldn't have gone five feet without tripping over roots.

Another crack. Was it off to the left?

Silence.

Then the unmistakable slide-and-click sound of a shotgun.

I turned slowly.

It was pointed right at us.

16

"WHAT IN A GATOR'S DREAM are you thinking?" Sawgrass Molly lowered the gun.

"We were—"

"Shh!" With the gun at her side, she reached out, grabbed my arm roughly, and pulled me through the brush. A weathered wooden shack stood in the middle of a clearing, leaning as if the lonely cracked window on one side might pull the whole thing to the ground.

"We were looking for you," I whispered as the others climbed through the weeds to join us.

Molly half laughed. She creaked open the door to the shack, disappeared inside, and came back with four bottles of water. "Here." She shook her head again. "Don't you think you have enough troubles without traipsing off into the swamp, in the dark, without supplies or any idea where you're going? How'd you even find me?"

"The crab traps," I said. "We remembered the traps you told

us about coming in. And we were careful." I felt defensive all of a sudden. "We stayed way clear of that alligator, Lou, and—"

Molly snorted. "Lou's the least of your troubles out here." The roar of an airboat, far away, mixed with the returning buzz of insects. "You get lost after dark, you're liable to run into poachers and drug runners and all manner of people who'll do you as much harm as the ones you're with at the clinic. I told you I was going to get you out of there, and I told you it needed to be done before anybody—"

"But you quit!" Sarah blurted. "We didn't know if you'd come back!"

"Who told you I quit?" Molly's eyes were fierce.

"Dr. Ames," Ben said.

Molly turned to Ben with narrowed eyes. "Your Dr. Ames," she said, "hustled me down to the dock soon as we walked out of that hangar, and the second he stepped off the boat in Everglades City, he fired me. Told me that if I came back, if I breathed one word about anything I'd seen—"

"Does he know you saw Trent?" I asked.

She paused. "I don't know. What I do know is that it's not safe for you to be here now." The roar of the airboat was getting louder. "You need to go back."

"Go back? Can't you take us?" Sarah sounded like a little kid.

Molly shook her head. "Dr. Ames has eyes all over this swamp, and he has connections. If dinnertime rolls around, and you're all missing, he'll have somebody after us before my boat's halfway to Everglades City. Like it or not, you need to return to the clinic and pretend everything's fine while I get things in place for later. Now get back there and act like the model patients you're supposed to be."

My stomach twisted. "But they're going to—"

"They're not doing anything tonight. In the morning, you'll be gone, and you'll be with people who can keep you safe." She stopped, listened hard to the sound of the boat. It was closer. She squatted in the dust and motioned for us to get down with her. "At midnight," she whispered, "you meet me at the docks. Bring nothing; if anyone sees you, it needs to look as if you've simply gone out to get some air. I'll have the boat, and I'll have help. We'll take you to a safe place, and *then* . . . once they can't get to you . . . *then* we'll let someone know what's going on." She looked at us, hard. "We get one chance at this. I don't care if you need to lie, break a window and run. . . . Do whatever you need to do to get there. *Midnight.*" Her eyes rested on Ben for a second. "*All* of you."

"What about Trent? And Kaylee?" I asked.

"I'll take care of them. You take care of yourselves." Suddenly, she stood, but she motioned for us to stay down while she listened. The airboat roar had died. "Go." She waved frantically down the path we'd come. "Get away from here quick as you can, and then get out your binoculars and start talking about all the birds you've seen and what a lovely paddle you had. I'll see you tonight."

The others started down the trail, but I didn't. I didn't want to leave. I'd known that something was wrong, but now, even *being* at the clinic felt dangerous.

"Go!" Molly shoved me roughly, and I stumbled and turned. "I'm afraid." My eyes burned with tears.

She didn't hug me like Mom would have, and her face didn't soften. If anything, it got harder, and her eyes burned darker. "You should be afraid. Now go."

17

TEN MINUTES BEFORE MIDNIGHT, I raised my hand to knock on Kaylee's door. I'd never seen her go in or out. I'd never even met her, but her chart was there at the door. So I knocked—even though the sign read DO NOT DISTURB.

I knew what the doctors had said about Kaylee—that her injury was more serious, so she'd take longer to recover. Now, I wondered if that was true, or if the treatment had made her worse.

I knocked again. Would Kaylee still be Kaylee when she opened the door? Or would I find a twelve-year-old Marie Curie inside her room instead?

I knocked once more, but there was no answer, and the door was locked.

"Molly said she'd take care of the others." Ben's voice was sharp, too loud for midnight.

"Shh." I stepped away from Kaylee's door. "I thought . . . I thought we should try."

Quentin and Sarah's doors opened at the same time. Quentin's hands were empty—*bring nothing*—and he looked lost, clenching them into fists at his sides. Sarah held her Frisbee.

"Seriously?" I hissed. "Tell me you don't think you're bringing that. I left my mom's photograph here. I left my clay birds and—"

"It's cover. In case we get caught, we can say she dragged us out to play," Quentin whispered. "Everybody ready?"

The outside air was heavy and thick when we opened the door. Our sneakers squished into the wet lawn.

It had rained after dinner. Ben had been playing badminton with Dr. Ames, and they came running for the door when the thunder rumbled, but by the time they got in, they were soaked, T-shirts dripping on the floor, and laughing. I don't know how Ben could stand to look at him across the net, talk with him as if everything was fine, but I guess it was a good thing. Dr. Ames had said good night to us like always and disappeared to his office.

"I don't hear anything," Quentin whispered as we approached the dock.

I heard things—but not what we were listening for. Not the roar of the airboat fan. Only our footsteps thumping quietly on the wood, the rising and falling of insect buzz, the rustle of dry grass—a raccoon or possum?—in the brush.

A light glowed in one window of the old hangar across the lawn. What was Trent building in there? Was he sleeping on that cot or working through the night? Did he remember that he used to be a Knicks fan from Queens who sculpted potato volcanoes and snorted milk out his nose? Did he remember holding Sarah's hand?

Thunder growled in the distance. Then there was a different rumble.

"Listen," I said. "She's coming."

It was an airboat. But as quickly as the sound had surfaced in the night air, it faded away. Whoever it was never came close to our dock.

"What time is it?" Sarah whispered.

"Quarter after," Ben said. "I bet she's not coming."

"She'll come." I remembered the intensity in her eyes, back at her beaten-down camp. I trusted her. She had to come.

The thunder grumbled closer. Lightning lit up the dock, flashed on the water, and rain pelted the kayaks with cold, plunking drops.

"I'm going in," Ben said. "I never should have agreed to this. That lady's a freak, and this whole thing is—"

"There you are!"

My heart almost stopped.

Dr. Ames hurried across the lawn, barefoot, wearing torn gym shorts and a faded red T-shirt. "Olga and Sergei came down to check on the monitoring equipment—the storm caused a power surge—and found your rooms empty. What are you *doing* out here? Don't you know that more people are struck by lightning in Florida than any other state?" He stepped toward us.

My breath froze in my chest, and I couldn't speak; I felt like I was suffocating, like he was squeezing all the air out of me, just by looking at me.

"Sorry, Dr. Ames." Sarah stepped forward and wiped her wet bangs from her eyes. "It was my idea; I thought it'd be awesome to get a game of midnight Frisbee going, and then when the rain started, we came down here to see the storm coming in over the water." Thunder clapped, and she jumped, then gave a sheepish grin. "I guess we weren't really thinking."

"Get on up to your rooms. We can't have you out in this storm." He waited until we all left the dock and followed us over the lawn. "Watch your step. It's slick out here with the mud." The rain was coming down harder, but the sound of an approaching airboat—anywhere even close—would have cut through it.

There was no airboat. There was nothing but rain and thunder and wind.

Midnight.

We get one chance at this.

Molly wasn't coming.

Dr. Ames held open the door to the clinic and shook his head. "You know your treatments are scheduled for first thing in the morning. Get to sleep or you'll be exhausted. It's after twelve thirty."

I stepped inside and looked back at the lake, boiling with fat raindrops, all around the empty dock.

Midnight.

We get one chance at this.

And it was over.

18

I DIDN'T SLEEP.

I couldn't.

I sat on the edge of the bed in my soaking wet clothes and stared out the window. The clinic lights were off, so there was nothing but dark except when lightning flashed, and the pond lit up, rainy green.

Why hadn't Molly come?

It was hard to imagine a storm stopping her, but maybe it held her up enough so that by the time she arrived, Dr. Ames was there. She would have had to turn away.

Where was she now?

What if she came back? What if she was there at the dock waiting?

I hadn't heard from Quentin or Sarah or Ben since my room door swung shut. Not a word. Not a knock.

They couldn't be asleep, could they? Should we try again?

I lifted myself from the bed slowly, so it wouldn't creak, and walked silently to the door. I pressed my ear to the crack.

The hallway was quiet.

I turned the knob and inched the door open.

"Did you need something?"

Dr. Ames sat in the hallway, lounging in a plush leather desk chair against the wall outside our rooms.

If my heart could have burst through my chest and run down the hallway, out into the pouring rain, it would have left me. But it stayed, frantic, pounding, while I answered.

"It's . . . I was a little hungry, so . . ."

"Cat, Cat, Cat . . . We simply can't have our patients running about at all hours of the night. What would your mother think?"

"I want to call my mom," I blurted. I'd never wanted anything more.

Dr. Ames looked at his watch. "At this hour? You'll scare her half to death. You can call her in the morning." He put his hands on the arms of his chair and pushed himself up. "You need your rest, kiddo. Are you having trouble sleeping?" He took another step toward me, put his hand on the edge of the door. "Because I could give you something for that."

"That's okay." I practically leaped back into my room. "I'm actually really tired. Thanks." I closed the door and stood with my back to it, my heart pulsing in my throat. I pushed in the lock, but it didn't matter. It couldn't keep me safe. Dr. Ames was in charge of all the keys. Dr. Ames was in charge of everything.

I couldn't breathe; I needed something—anything—to wipe away the image of his face outside my door. I picked up the bag of clay from my dresser, took out what was left, and kneaded it over and over in my hands until they stopped shaking.

I squeezed the clay, pulled and smoothed its surface. I tried to shape an osprey, but it didn't work. I started over and over, but every time I thought I might have its shape, the soaring feel of its wings, I'd hold up the clay to look and realize it was all wrong. All wrong.

Tears streamed down my face onto the big, ugly gray lump of bird and made it all slimy, and I gave up. I squeezed as hard as I could, until both my hands ached and the clay oozed between my fingers.

I flung the clay to the floor, crossed the room to the window, and looked out. The night was silent and quiet and dark.

Slowly, I flipped the latch and I pushed up on the sill. My clay-streaked fingers left gray smudges, but the window opened without a sound. There was the tiniest click when I pushed out the screen, caught it, and lowered it to the ground outside.

I heard a cell phone ring in the hallway, and I froze. I could hear Dr. Ames's voice, but not his words. I wanted to go to the door and listen. But more than that, I wanted to get away.

Lightning illuminated the lawn, the pond, and the never-ending swamp beyond, the river of grass and snakes, poachers and drug runners. And Molly. Somewhere. Could I find her?

I pushed the window up as high as it would go and leaned my head out into the rain.

The clinic's exterior lights came on and flooded the night with light. Sergei stood patrol on the sidewalk, wrapped in rain gear as if he'd be there all night. Were they all part of this? The orderlies and Elena the chef? Did they all know? Or were they simply carrying out the duties on their clipboards?

It didn't matter. Even if Sergei didn't know the truth, I couldn't tell him. He wouldn't understand me, and if I tried to run, he'd take me straight to Dr. Ames.

I brought my head inside and closed the window.

There was no way I could get past him.

Still in my wet clothes, I curled up on top of the bedspread, knees tucked tightly into my chest. I didn't sleep.

I stayed that way until the rain stopped and the sun rose over the trees.

19

IT WAS AFTER THE SUN came up—almost six thirty—when I heard the door next to mine open and close. I rushed to my door but hesitated to open it. Would Dr. Ames still be waiting there, watching?

But the footsteps were quieter, softer than his. I opened the door.

Quentin stood in the hallway, hovering between my door and Sarah's as if he were afraid to knock on either one, afraid a monster might pop out. But the monster was gone—he'd crept away sometime during the night while I lay there, not sleeping, in my room. The coffee mug next to his chair was empty, too.

"We need to get everyone together," I whispered to Quentin, "and then we need to—"

"Good morning!" Dr. Ames called down the hallway. He'd emerged from his office, briefcase slung over his shoulder and—was that a rolling suitcase behind him?

I looked at Quentin and made a fast decision; we had to pretend everything was fine.

"Good morning, Dr. Ames." I tried to make my voice relax. "Sorry about last night. I guess we were kind of dumb."

"Well, kids will be kids." He walked up to us and parked his suitcase as Sarah and Ben joined us in the hallway. Sarah was still in her sweatpants and T-shirt, but Ben was dressed like he might have been going to school. "Oh good," Dr. Ames said. "Since you're all together, I need to talk with you about today." He took a deep breath, then looked from Ben to Sarah to Quentin to me. Was he trying to decide who to call into the lab? Who did he want to "change" first? It felt like we were standing in the path of an oncoming train with nowhere to go.

Dr. Ames let out his breath in a big whoosh. "I know we'd planned on moving forward with your treatment today, but there's been an issue with funding for the clinic."

"Oh," Quentin said. "So there's . . . a delay?" I could almost see the thoughts churning behind his brown eyes. What did that mean? Was it even true? Would we have more time? Enough to escape?

"No." Dr. Ames shook his head, and my heart sank. We wouldn't have more time. The train was coming for us, and there was nowhere to—

"I'm afraid the project has been discontinued," Dr. Ames said. He gave a sad smile and shrugged. "You're going home."

"We are?" Sarah's eyes lit up.

"When?" Quentin asked.

Dr. Ames looked at his watch. "Soon." He adjusted the briefcase over his shoulder and grabbed the handle of his suitcase. "Pack your things right after breakfast. We'll have a boat waiting at the dock to take you to Everglades City, and from there, you'll take a van to Miami. We've already called your families, and they'll be flying in tonight to meet you at the airport."

"But this is so quick! What about our treatment?" Quentin asked. His voice was bursting with questions, but that was the only one he asked aloud.

Dr. Ames sighed. "It's been a long time coming, I'm sad to say. I thought we'd be able to hold on a few more weeks, but that's not to be. Hopefully, our funding situation will improve down the road, and perhaps we'll be able to have you back."

I shivered.

"But for now," he continued, "the clinic is shutting down." He pulled his suitcase down the hall toward the door. "Get some breakfast," he called over his shoulder. "Pack your things, and take headache medicine if you need it. We'll be leaving the docks at nine." He walked out the door, and we watched through the window as he stopped along the sidewalk to talk with Dr. Gunther.

"Dr. Gunther looks way more upset about the clinic closing than Dr. Ames," Sarah said. Dr. Gunther's gray-white eyebrows knit together over his eyes as if they'd never come apart, and his hands flew through the air as he spoke to Dr. Ames.

"This is Dr. Gunther's whole life," Ben scoffed. "He's nothing without this place."

Quentin turned to him. "How do you know so much about Dr. Gunther?"

Ben shrugged. "Dr. Ames tells me lots of stuff."

"And you trust Dr. Ames?" I scoffed. "He's the one who—"

"Shh!" Quentin glared at me. I didn't blame him; I'd heard

my own voice rising. I couldn't help it. "Don't be stupid. Not when we're this close to going home."

"Our cell phones will work in Everglades City, right?" Sarah's voice was full of life. "I'm calling my mom the second I have service."

"She'll be on the plane, probably," I said. But my voice sounded weak, even to me. None of this made sense. When had Dr. Ames called our parents? Early this morning? What could have happened to change everything from the time he stopped me outside my door? He wouldn't let me call Mom until morning. Had he then gone and called her himself? And told her to come get me? It didn't make sense. And I was pretty sure you couldn't even get a flight from the West Coast on such short notice and make it to Miami the same day.

I looked back out the window. There were two airboats tied to the dock. Dr. Gunther was gone—I didn't see where—but Dr. Ames was talking with another man on the dock, and neither of them looked happy. The man looked familiar, but from the window, I couldn't tell why. And there wasn't time.

"Who's that guy?" Sarah asked.

"Never seen him." Quentin frowned. "And what's the second airboat? It's not Molly's."

"I don't know." I'd taken medicine, but it wasn't fending off my headache. I pressed my hands to my temples. "One boat's to take us to Everglades City, I guess. *If* he's telling the truth." I hadn't meant to say that aloud, but I did.

"Of course he's telling the truth," Ben blurted. "Where else would we be going?" I stared at him. While I felt all confused and tied in knots, he looked happier than I'd ever seen him. And it felt wrong. Ben had *wanted* to be here so he could get well and ride horses again. Now, he didn't even seem to care that the clinic was shutting down.

If that was the truth. My mind couldn't let go of that *if*. I couldn't get on that boat without knowing more.

I turned to Quentin. "We need to get into Dr. Ames's office."

He didn't argue. "But what about Gunther?" Dr. Gunther hadn't come back into the clinic, and we couldn't see him out the window. Was he in the hangar with Trent, helping him pack up his laboratory? Or with Kaylee, getting her ready to leave? It didn't matter.

"I'm going." I started down the hall to Dr. Ames's office. I didn't care if no one followed me. I needed to know the truth.

20

IT WAS ALMOST TOO EASY to find.

When the four of us got to Dr. Ames's office, the door was wide open. His laptop computer was there on the desk, with his e-mail program open, the most recent message right there on the screen, dated last night.

Sender: R. J. Wiley
Recipient: Mark W. Ames
Subject: Moscow

Mark,

As we discussed tonight, the risk associated with continuing the Everglades project is too great at this point. We can still contain the public relations damage if we let Fish & Wildlife nail Gunther for possession of endandered species. Let that be the reason we shut down. The clinic dies, but the project lives on with Narayev in Russia. He can complete work on the remaining subjects and launch the next step from there. In the morning, we'll move forward with plans to explain the disappearance of the subjects.

I've scheduled an 11 am charter plane for tomorrow. Private Sky Jets operates out of Miami International Airport, and your confirmation number is 472BRQ. Please note that you will need to provide identification for the following passengers listed for the flight:

There was his name at the bottom of the screen.

Ames, Mark

"Just him?" Sarah whispered. I could feel her breath on my shoulder. "I thought Dr. Gunther was going, too."

"Scroll down." Quentin reached past me to the mouse and scrolled until we could see the full list. Dr. Gunther's name still wasn't there. But our names were.

Grayson, Catherine
Hayes, Quentin
Jacobsen, Sarah
McCain, Benjamin
Perkins, Trent

All of us, except for Kaylee. On a list of passengers leaving for Moscow in a few hours.

I sucked in my breath. I couldn't move, except to shake my head. It was too awful, too surreal to be true. But there it was.

"We're not going home," Quentin whispered. "We're going to Russia."

"What?" Ben tried to push Quentin out of the way to see. "That's crazy." He leaned in to the screen. "This is an airplane charter reservation," he said weakly. "It doesn't mean anything. It could be a research trip for Dr. Gunther now that he's done here, or—"

"Ben," Quentin said, his voice rising. "Our names are on that passenger list."

"No . . . no." Sarah's eyes filled with tears and fear, all at once. She'd felt all along something was wrong, longer than any of us. But this morning, for a few minutes, she'd believed she was going home.

I put a hand on her arm, maybe to make her feel better, maybe to steady myself. "We can still think of something. We were close to getting away before, and we—"

"We're out of time! We're leaving in, like, an hour." Sarah was choking back sobs. "They're not going to let us near the boats before then. We'll never escape!"

"Maybe not right now." Quentin's jaw muscle twitched, and his eyes flashed, angry. "But somewhere along the way, somewhere on that boat or getting into the van, we may have a chance to run. We need to *make* that chance. We need to stay together and stay ready." His eyes moved from Sarah, to me, to Ben, as if he could weave a knot to bind us all together.

"The phone!" Sarah lunged for it. "I'm calling my mom and dad." But when she pressed the buttons, there was some recording, and she dropped it to the desk, crying. "There's a stupid password."

"We can e-mail, though!" Quentin leaned over the computer,

just as a voice drifted through the open window. I peered out, careful to stay out of sight, and saw Dr. Ames hurrying up from the dock as one of the airboats pushed off into the water. "He's coming! We have to go!"

"Hold on!" Quentin was almost pounding on the keys. "I can't get this to open a new message!"

"There's no time!" I pulled at Quentin's arm, and we hurried for the door.

"We never saw this. We can't let on that we know anything," I said, looking back.

But Ben wasn't coming. He'd stayed at the desk, squinting at the screen as if he still couldn't understand.

"Let's go!" I hissed, and he jumped as if he'd been someplace else. He rushed to the door and looked back at Dr. Ames's desk before he followed us down the hall toward the cafeteria.

Dr. Ames was waiting there with a stack of white cardboard boxes. "Sorry to rush you," he said, "but the van's meeting us earlier than I thought, so we need to get going." He pressed a boxed breakfast into each of our hands. "Bagels, cream cheese, and a banana for the ride," he said. "Get packed and bring it with you, okay? Meet at the boat in ten minutes."

"Ten minutes!" Sarah's mouth hung open, and I saw tears welling in her eyes again. She couldn't let on that we knew.

"It's okay," I said quickly, and put an arm around her. "I don't have much stuff," I joked, "so I'll help you pack your Frisbees."

Quentin followed us, but Ben lingered and said something to Dr. Ames.

"You coming?" Quentin called.

"Yeah, but . . ." He turned to Dr. Ames. "I'm allergic to bananas. Can I get something else?"

Dr. Ames put an arm around Ben's shoulders and waved us on. "Let me get this guy something he can eat, and I'll send him right down."

"Great," Quentin said tightly, and turned down the hallway, but then stopped. I knew he was worried about what Ben might tell Dr. Ames. So was I, but what could we do? Nothing.

"Everything okay?" Dr. Ames smiled at the rest of us, that same warm smile he'd flashed when Mom and I arrived. "Go on and get packed. I know it sounds like a long morning of travel, but you'll be back with your families in no time."

I nodded and followed Quentin toward our rooms, but I had to look back at Dr. Ames once more. I'd never seen anyone lie so well.

21

BEN WAS ALREADY AT THE dock when we got there. He had a duffel bag, the one he'd had back in Everglades City that first day, when his aunt was there and Mom was there with me. Back when I was nervous for all the wrong reasons.

Trent was at the dock, too, already on the boat. How would Dr. Ames explain that, when he'd told us Trent had gone home?

Trent sat right next to the driver's chair with a bag at his feet, his fingers busy with a tiny screwdriver and some kind of gauge or something, maybe part of the navigation stuff from the old plane in the hangar. His eyes moved back and forth from the boat's controls to the mess of electronics in his lap.

"Hey," I said. "Remember me? From breakfast that day?"

He looked up and blinked once. "Indeed, I do. I've made tremendous progress with the alternating current since then." He went back to fiddling with the mess of wires and panels in his hands.

There was a splash to our right, and I turned to see a blue

heron gulping down a frog or fish. It was so close I could see the way the water beaded as it dripped down sleek blue-gray feathers.

Trent reached for something in his bag and startled the heron. I watched it take off, pumping its wings, and wished I could fly away, too.

What would happen to us if we couldn't escape? Would I recognize a great blue heron a week from now? A month from now? Or would I turn into Marie Curie or one of those other scientists and be like Trent, focused on some scientific problem that got planted in my head? I watched him bite his lip in concentration as he turned the gauge over in his hands.

We *had* to escape. Because looking at Trent, I knew if they took me away and finished their project, even if Mom and Dad found me one day, I'd never be *me* again.

Dr. Ames walked down the path with a scruffy guy who was easily half a foot taller than he was and twice as wide. "Great, you're all right on time," Dr. Ames said, "and I see that you're getting reacquainted with Trent. As you know, he'd gone home, but he'd come back to us for additional treatment this week. It's so unfortunate that we've had this funding issue." He shook his head.

"Where's Kaylee?" I asked. She hadn't been on the plane list from his office either. What happened to her?

"She's not feeling well, Cat—as you know, her injury was more severe than yours, and she's still suffering debilitating headaches. You know how loud these airboats can be, so her parents have decided to arrange for a medical helicopter instead. She'll be picked up later on."

A lump swelled in my throat, but I nodded and didn't say

anything. It felt like letting Lucy send Amberlee away all over again, only worse. A thousand times worse. How could we leave Kaylee behind? What would happen to her? What kind of person would just nod and let this happen? What kind of person was I?

"All right." Dr. Ames looked down at our bags, heaped up in that open space on the boat's deck. "Got everything?"

Somebody must have nodded.

"Great." He smiled and climbed onto the boat, and the man with him climbed into the seat at the control panel. Trent immediately leaned over to investigate the boat's switches and panels. When Dr. Ames pulled out the boat's operations manual and handed it to Trent, his face lit up like Christmas morning and he immediately started reading.

I hadn't seen this airboat driver from the window; I'd hoped, somehow, Molly would be back. But instead we had this guy— young and muscular, with a tattooed vine that curled around his neck and down his shoulder and disappeared under a torn white T-shirt. He reached under his seat, pulled a thermos from an oversize duffel bag, and took a long drink from it while Dr. Ames helped us onto the boat. Unzipped, the driver's bag flopped open, and inside, I could see a big handheld floodlight, ropes, and a thick, rusted metal hook. The airboat floor was smeared with brown-red stains that I didn't even want to think about. Best case scenario: he might have been an alligator poacher. But I knew from Molly's warnings that worse things went on in the swamp.

I found my voice again. "Isn't Dr. Gunther coming?" His name hadn't been on the charter plane list either.

"He's finishing up some work at the clinic." Did I imagine it? Or did Dr. Ames's eyes darken? "He'll join us later."

I had more questions, but the boat guy—he never said hello or told us his name—started up the giant propeller fan, and we left. We zipped through channels, past the shacks in the mangroves, past the spot where One-Eyed Lou should have been guarding her babies, but I didn't see her. The boat must have scared her off. The roar of the engine never let up; we didn't get earplugs this time, and my head was pounding.

This driver was no Sawgrass Molly. He never looked up at the osprey nests, never slowed to peer into the tangled grass along the banks and search for gator babies. And he looked like he wanted to swat Trent, who was leaning over, studying every press of a button and flick of a switch at the control panel.

The driver maneuvered the boat through the river's grassy bends as fast as he could without running it up on the mud banks. This trip was happening too fast. Once we got to Everglades City, once they locked us in that van, there would be no chance to escape.

Quentin sat up straighter as we approached the mouth of the river, where it opened up into wider waters. He switched seats so he was next to me, staring up into a cypress on my side of the boat as if he'd moved to search for eagle or osprey nests, and he leaned in close. "What if we jump?"

"Now?" I watched the water rushing by. I couldn't tell how deep it was; there were no reeds, no grasses I could see. Nothing to reassure me. "Where would we go?"

He pointed to the shoreline, maybe fifty yards to our left. It was thick with brush, but a thin brown trail snaked up from the water's edge and disappeared into the green. Could we make it that far? Could everyone swim? Sarah probably could—there didn't seem to be a sport she didn't love—but I had no idea about Ben. And Trent? Trent wouldn't even acknowledge we were there, so it wasn't likely he'd jump into the river if we told him to. We couldn't leave him.

I looked at the long stretch of water and shook my head. "We'd never make it there before they reached us in the boat."

Dr. Ames looked back over his shoulder at us, and Quentin craned his neck to search the treetops again. He pointed up, and I followed the line of his arm. There was nothing there.

"Keep looking that way," he half shouted into my ear. The engine was so loud there was no way anyone else could hear him. "I think we could do it. I'm pretty sure airboats can't go in reverse. And the river's pretty narrow here; he couldn't turn around easily. It might take long enough that we could—"

As if the boat itself could hear our plans, it shot forward. I grabbed a railing to catch myself and looked up. While Trent fumbled to retrieve the screwdriver he dropped, the driver pushed the throttle as far as he could. Apparently, the river was plenty wide here to open it up and fly.

I looked at Quentin. Any chance we had at jumping from the boat was gone.

In less than a minute, the boat slowed, and we pulled up to an empty dock in Everglades City. Dr. Ames stood over us while the driver tossed a line around a barnacle-crusted post.

Sarah hurried over to Quentin and me—maybe hoping we'd thought of something. Or maybe she felt better being close. Ben lingered at the bow of the boat, staring into the swamp as if he'd simply given up. Maybe he was the smart one.

"All right." Dr. Ames stepped onto the weathered dock and reached out to us. I had to force myself not to shrink back.

I reached up for his hand. "Thanks." Sarah and Ben and Quentin climbed off the boat, too. The dock was small, and it kept wobbling under my feet. Dr. Ames caught my arm to steady me. I wanted to shove him away and run, but I didn't.

"Balance is often the last thing to come back." His mouth smiled, but his eyes didn't. They looked past me. I turned to follow his gaze and watched a dark-blue van with tinted windows kicking up dust on the gravel-dirt road as it approached the dock.

"Let's go, Trent." Dr. Ames waited while Trent reluctantly left the boat's control panel and climbed onto the dock.

"Thanks." Dr. Ames pressed a fifty-dollar bill into the boat driver's hand. "Perfect timing." Gravel crunched as the blue van pulled up next to us. "Our ride is here."

22

DR. AMES FLUNG OUR BAGS on top of some big crates in the back of the van and slammed down the rear hatch. He slid open the side door and stood, waiting.

Trent wouldn't leave his backpack full of electronics in the back. He scurried up the steps, clutching it to his chest, and scrambled into the far back. There were four rows—two bucket seats in the front, then two small benches, with room for people to get in and out by the sliding door, and a long bench stretching across the back of the van. Trent slid across that long bench, unzipped his bag, spread out all his tools and wires, and went back to work.

I stood frozen at the door.

"Cat?" Dr. Ames raised his eyebrows.

My throat tightened. Everything was closing in on me, and it was only when I felt Quentin's hand on my shoulder that I could say anything at all. "I . . . feel a little sick from the airboat ride," I said. "Is there someplace I can get water?"

I knew there wasn't. I didn't want to get in that van.

Dr. Ames frowned. "Headache? You took medicine this morning, didn't you?"

"Yes. My head's okay. I'm just queasy."

"The airboat was never a problem for you before."

"That guy drove faster."

He nodded, then gave a tight smile. "I'm afraid this luxury waterfront property is a bit lacking in facilities." He swung an arm out at the empty gravel parking lot. "We'll stop and get you something to drink once we're on the road."

"Okay." But I didn't move. Climbing in that van felt like climbing into a coffin. "Can you give me a minute? A little fresh air and I'll be fine, probably." I stepped back and tried to breathe. I wanted to run, but there was nowhere to go.

Ben climbed in and sat on the bench behind the driver's seat. He turned his whole body toward the window.

Quentin stepped up next and sat behind Ben. Sarah sat next to Quentin on the middle bench.

Dr. Ames crossed his arms in front of him. "Cat?"

I blinked hard, once, and climbed up next to Ben. Dr. Ames slammed the door, and the thump shook my whole body, straight to my heart. I forced myself to take a deep breath. And coughed.

"It smells like my hockey bag in here," Sarah said behind me as Dr. Ames climbed into the front passenger seat.

I'd never smelled a hockey bag, but if they smelled like dirty, wet clothes left to mildew in the heat, then Sarah was right. There was stale cigarette smoke, too, and something else, pungent and sweet. None of it was helping my clenched-up stomach.

The driver pressed a button and his window closed; he flicked on the air-conditioning, and cooler air poured out from the vents in front. "That any better?" His voice was as rough as the dusty road. I leaned forward to see him, but his face was shaded by a red baseball cap, pulled down low. The skin I could see in the shadows was leathered and tan. He reached for the gearshift with a hand marked with sun spots, scratches, and dried mud.

We didn't talk. There was no airboat engine to drown out our whispers. The radio was off, the only sound a quiet rush of air-conditioning that was only halfway reaching the backseats.

We pulled out of the long gravel driveway onto a paved road just as Dr. Ames's cell phone rang. I leaned forward and saw GUNTHER on the screen before he pressed the phone to his ear. "What is it?"

I couldn't make out exact words, but I could hear the rise and fall of Dr. Gunther's voice on the other end. He was talking fast.

"You will make the calls *exactly* as we discussed," Dr. Ames said into the phone, his voice rising, "and you'll do it in . . ." He pushed the sleeve of his windbreaker up over his watch, then looked at the van's driver. "How long? Thirty minutes?" The driver gave a quick nod.

"Get it done, Rudolph." Dr. Ames clicked a button on top of his phone and dropped it into his lap.

What calls? Get what done? Hadn't they already called our parents and told lies? Told them we were coming home?

I twisted in my seat and stole a glance at Quentin. He was looking out the window, frowning.

The van sped up, past roadside stands advertising airboat rides and pictures taken with baby alligators, power lines that seemed to go nowhere, dried-out ditches crisscrossed with animal tracks in what was left of the mud. The landscape didn't look any different than it had when Mom and I drove into town from the airport.

How could that have been only a week ago? It felt like so much longer. And that life back home that I'd been so anxious to fix, to change . . . I'd give anything now to have it back, concussion and messed-up friendships and all. I wanted the chance to make things right, with Amberlee, and Lucy, and with myself. I wanted to go home so badly it was all I could do not to curl up on the floor of the van and cry.

I breathed in. And got a big gulp of smoke, thicker than we'd smelled out in the swamp.

I turned to Quentin, leaned back, and raised my eyebrows. He came forward and rested his arms on his knees.

"Can you smell that?" I whispered.

He nodded. "Fires must be closer."

I turned to face forward. Dr. Ames had lowered his visor and was peering back at us in the mirror.

I met his eyes, straight on. "How long until we get there?"

"Miami's still about ninety minutes away," he said.

"I thought you said thirty minutes." My heart felt like it was racing around my chest, looking for a way out. I knew Miami was more than half an hour away. Where were we *really* going?

"Oh, that. We . . . uh . . . may need to take a slight detour if the roads are blocked off because of wildfires. But don't worry. I'm sure Gus knows some shortcuts."

Traffic slowed in front of us, and Gus's hands clenched on the steering wheel. His shortcuts apparently didn't keep us from getting stuck in traffic. Cars in front of us crawled along. Who was in those cars? Anyone who could help us?

I turned to Quentin. "Want to play the alphabet game?"

"What?" He looked at me as if I'd lost my mind. "Now?"

"Yes, now." My eyes narrowed. "Lean up; you'll be able to see better."

He hesitated, but I reached back and pulled his hand until he was leaned over the seat, just inches from my face. "See? There! On that sign—GAS-FOOD-CAMPING—I got an A." I leaned so close my nose brushed his hair, and I whispered, "Should we try to jump out while traffic is stopped?"

He nodded slowly. "Maybe," he whispered, then shouted, "B! Boat launch!"

In front, Dr. Ames poked at his cell phone.

"We'd have to all go at once," Quentin whispered. He pulled Sarah up next to him and leaned over, his mouth to her ear. I watched her eyes get wide. He whispered to her again.

Dr. Ames was watching in the mirror.

"I got B, another boat launch!" I said loudly. "Plus C, Camping, and D, Road Work Ahead."

"Is that why we slowed down?" Quentin called up to the front. "Construction?"

"No." Gus's hands were tight on the steering wheel. "It's a roadblock."

"For what?" I asked.

"Nothing to worry about," Dr. Ames said, but he was looking at Gus—not us. "Stay cool. I'll get us through."

Police lights flashed five or six cars ahead of us. Gus kept looking in the rearview mirror. He was having trouble staying cool. How come?

"You said this job would be quick and easy." Gus put the van in park—traffic had come to a complete stop—and turned his body toward Dr. Ames. "What if they look in back?"

"Shh!" Dr. Ames growled, and even though he was half Gus's size, Gus backed off. "I told you, we're fine. Just drive."

"E, Exit nineteen!" I shouted, and turned back to Quentin and Sarah. "If we jump out, we can bang on somebody's car window . . . and . . ."

Quentin shook his head. "And tell them that one of the most well-respected clinics in the country has kidnapped us?" he hissed. "We'd be back in this van, buckled in our seat belts so fast it'd make—"

Sarah interrupted him. "D! Speed Limit sixty-five." She leaned closer to us. "He was looking again."

Dr. Ames's cell phone rang as we pulled up to the flashing lights.

Quentin looked longingly at the police cars. "Maybe we could . . ."

"No. Remember what Molly said about the police around here? We can't take that chance." I took a deep breath.

Four cars—two sheriff's vehicles, a U.S. Fish and Wildlife SUV, and a van that said DRUG ENFORCEMENT AGENCY—lined the shoulders of the road.

Gus tugged the brim of his baseball hat and cursed under his breath.

"Stay cool," Dr. Ames growled. His phone kept ringing, but he ignored it as a sheriff's deputy motioned for Gus to roll down the van's window.

"Morning," the deputy said. "We need you to turn right on the county road up ahead. Fire's taken a turn in this wind, and we can't have anybody in its path."

"No problem, sir." Gus wiped sweat from his nose, even thought the AC was blasting inside the van.

Dr. Ames leaned toward the driver's window and gave a small wave. "We're transporting some patients from I-CAN, the head-injury clinic, sir. Don't want to put them in any danger, so we appreciate the heads-up."

The sheriff's deputy peered into the backseats and paused.

"All righty. Pull over up here," he said. "Ted will have a quick look in the back and then you can go ahead."

"Excuse me, sir? Ah . . . Ted?" Dr. Ames's voice was tight, his smile forced.

"They're running a DEA checkpoint while we're set up." The sheriff's deputy shrugged. "Two birds with one stone, I suppose. I'm sure he'll wave you right through."

Gus gave Dr. Ames a panicked look, but he put the van in gear and pulled ahead to the next set of flashing lights.

I don't know how I knew—but all of a sudden, it all came together in my head: Molly's warnings of drug runners in the swamp, the funny smell in the van, the crates in the back. I leaned close to Quentin. "He's got drugs in here," I whispered.

His eyes flashed with shock—and then with knowing. They darted to the seat behind him, where Trent hadn't even looked

· · · 156 · · ·

up, and behind that, where our bags hid whatever was in the crates underneath. He nodded.

"I think we should run." The words were easy to say, but my body was afraid to move.

"Run where?" Sarah clutched Quentin's arm so hard her fingernails dug into his flesh. "What about our stuff?"

I looked over my shoulder. All our bags were heaped in the back of the van. My clay birds were probably already crushed. And none of it would matter if we couldn't get away. "We leave it."

Dr. Ames started talking into his phone again. "R. J.?" His voice was urgent. "We're at a roadblock. No, no. A *real* roadblock with federal agents. I need you to get us through!"

"Who's R. J.?" Sarah hissed in my ear. "And how's he going to get us through?"

I turned and whispered, "It must be R. J. Wiley, that guy from the e-mail. He's a senator or something, Molly said, and Dr. Ames is related to him."

"Well, you'd bloody well better be able to call them off." Dr. Ames glanced over his shoulder and must have seen us staring because he lowered his voice and turned up the radio, and we couldn't hear the rest. But his attention was divided. Our chance was now.

"We should run," I whispered again.

"*Where?*" Sarah nudged Quentin. She looked at me. "To the police?"

I shook my head. "We can't. Not yet."

Gus had pulled the van forward to the DEA car. He slammed the gear shift into park, leaned back, and glared at Dr. Ames.

Then he rolled down the window and smiled. "Morning, officer."

"Step out of the van, please."

Dr. Ames leaned over. "I'm sorry, officer, but we're from the International Center for Advanced Neurology, and we have some young head-injury patients in the back. Their conditions are rather fragile, and we need to get them to Miami, so if—"

"I didn't say for *them* to step out of the van." The officer lowered his mirrored sunglasses and gazed in through the window. "I said for *you* to step out."

Dr. Ames nodded quickly at Gus, and they opened their doors. A second DEA officer was at Dr. Ames's side as soon as he stepped down from the van.

"Ready?" Quentin whispered, reaching for Sarah's hand next to him.

But she pulled back. "*Where?*" she said again, and shook her head. "Into the swamp? We're safe right now." She gestured out the window, where Dr. Ames was talking with the DEA officer. "Nothing's going to happen to us with all these cops around."

"But what if the police let them go?" Quentin whispered.

Dr. Ames's phone dinged in the front seat—he hadn't taken it out with him—and I leaned forward. "It's his voice mail." I looked out the window. Dr. Ames was still talking with one officer, while the other headed toward the back of the van with Gus behind him. Gus had taken off his hat, and sweat soaked his hair. I reached between the seats and grabbed the phone.

Ben turned away from the window. "Don't do that," he warned. "You're going to get us in trouble."

"You don't think we're already in trouble?" I snapped.

"Hurry up!" Quentin whispered.

I pressed the voice mail button and waited.

"Ames," the voice said. It was so quiet, so tight it sounded like it might break in two. "It's done."

"It's Dr. Gunther," I said.

"What'd he say?" Quentin asked.

"Wait!" I held the phone out from my ear a little so they could lean in and hear, too.

"It's done," Dr. Gunther said again, and this time, his voice shuddered. "God help me, I did it; I called them. I got through to all the parents—and I told them . . ." He choked on a sob. "I told them the kids are dead."

23

EVERYTHING HAPPENED AT ONCE.

Before we could process what we'd heard, the back hatch flew open, the DEA officer called for backup—"Dan, over here!"— and Gus shoved the officer hard, face-first, into the rear door of the van and took off running into the woods.

We knelt on the seats staring back, even Trent. Dr. Ames rushed to the back of the van. We caught snatches of his frantic conversation with the DEA officer, who was holding his hand to his bloody nose.

"... have no idea how this could have happened ... hired through a car service ... can't imagine ..."

Whatever he said, it wasn't good enough. The DEA officer grabbed Dr. Ames roughly by the arm as the other officer arrived at the back of the van.

The chance we'd hoped for—the chance we thought we'd never get—was here.

I pulled on Quentin's shirt. "Now!" It shook him out of the

spell of the drama unfolding behind us. I tugged Ben's sleeve—
"Come on, let's go!"—and reached for the handle of the side
door.

It was locked.

"Hit the unlock button!" I motioned for Ben to reach up
between the seat and the front driver's door, but he didn't move.
I figured he was in shock—so much had happened—so I climbed
up and did it myself.

I pulled the handle, and this time, the side door slid open. I
lowered myself to the ground and crouched beside the van, motioning for Quentin and Sarah to get down, get hidden. "Grab his
phone! Come on!"

Quentin shoved Dr. Ames's phone into his pocket and jumped
down. "Ben, come on! We need to get out of here!" Behind the van,
Dr. Ames faced away from us, talking with the DEA officers. The
one officer had let go of his arm and was nodding. "Ben, let's *go!*"

"I don't think we should do this," Ben said. "What if—"

"We have to go *now*!" I pleaded. "Come on!"

Ben looked over his shoulder, out the back of the van—then
at us. Finally, he bit his lip, squinted, slid across the seat, and
jumped from the van.

"Shh!" I pulled Ben lower and crept toward the back of the
van. One of the DEA officers was on his cell phone, nodding. He
handed the phone to Dr. Ames, who didn't look worried at all
anymore. Had he convinced them everything was fine? Had Senator Wiley somehow called off the police? I could barely talk; my
throat was full of my pounding heart and dust and fear, but I
reached out, pulled in Quentin and Sarah and Ben, and whispered

what I knew we had to do, even though it felt impossible. "We have to run. Into the swamp!"

Sarah's face lit up with panic. "We can't just—"

"Yes, we can! We have to!"

"But the police—"

Quentin grabbed her shoulder and spun her around. "Sarah, look!"

One of the DEA officers stood next to Dr. Ames, laughing as he pulled our bags from the van. Then he lugged the crates out, lined them up on the road, put the luggage back inside, and slammed the door closed. Dr. Ames stood, shaking his head, as the officer pried off the top of a crate to reveal a cube of leafy deep-green plants, wilted and packed together.

For now, the officers were focused on the drugs, but that would change when they realized the sick kids had run off. Then they'd be after us, to get us back to "safety." To Dr. Ames.

"Come on," I whispered, creeping toward the front of the van with Quentin ahead of me. "If we can run behind that DEA car, there's thick brush at the edge of the road. We'll have a chance to disappear."

"It'll never work," Ben said. "They'll come after us."

"We have to try." I followed Quentin, nearly suffocating in the wet, smoky air.

He whispered over his shoulder. "If they stay busy long enough, we can get away. We can—"

"Molly!" I forgot to whisper. Quentin froze, but the crowd gathered at the back of the van now had pried the lid off another, even fuller crate of drugs. "We can go back and find Molly," I whispered. "She'll help us."

"She ditched us once already," Ben said, looking back at the van as if he were having second thoughts about leaving at all.

I looked back, too, and saw a shadow move in the van. We weren't all out. "Trent."

Quentin winced but nodded. We had to get him; we had to at least try.

"Wait here," I glanced back—a National Guard truck had pulled up behind the police vehicles, and Dr. Ames had walked back to talk with the soldiers. Were they here for the drugs? Or was the fire so bad they were called in for that? There wasn't time to worry about it.

"Trent?" I climbed back in the van.

He looked up.

"It's time to go."

He frowned. "I'm finishing up a circuit right now, so I'll be unavailable for another hour or so."

I wanted to scream at him, to pull those stupid wires and batteries from his hands and throw them in his face, but none of this was Trent's fault.

"I'm sorry. But we have to leave right now." I could see Dr. Ames down the road; he gestured toward the van, and my heart froze. But the other vehicles blocked his view of the side where Quentin, Ben, and Sarah were hiding. Dr. Ames couldn't see them, couldn't know what was happening.

"You have to come with us," I told Trent, lowering my voice. "You're in danger. We all are, and we have to get away. It's the only way we'll ever get to go home. You want to go home, right?"

He looked confused, as if he couldn't quite remember home.

"Trent, remember living in Queens? In New York City? You

lived there with your foster parents and your little brother." What had Sarah said his name was? "Jason! Remember Jason? He needs you, and you need to come with us so we can get home. Okay?"

Trent didn't respond, but his mouth twitched, and his eyes welled up with tears. Somewhere, the old Trent was still in there, buried alive under someone else's DNA and artificial memories. He took a deep breath, then shook his head as if my words simply hadn't made sense.

"You have to come with me," I said again.

He looked down at his mess of wires and motors. "I seem to be missing a part. I need to get back to the workshop to bring this project to completion."

"That's where we're going!" If that was what it took . . . "Back to the workshop. But we have to get out and walk. That's what Dr. Ames said."

Trent blinked, but he started gathering his things, stuffing them into his bag. I looked out the rear window. Dr. Ames had his hand at his eyes, shading them from the sun as he looked toward the van.

"Can you do that faster?" I reached for a handful of wires, but he held up an arm to block me.

"These components must be kept in order," he said calmly.

"Okay, okay. But hurry!" I pulled my hand back. I had to keep him happy, keep him from drawing attention. I tried to slow my breathing, but Dr. Ames had started back toward the van. I looked out the side window; Quentin, Sarah, and Ben were still crouched, sweaty and scared. "Ready?"

"I believe that's everything." Trent zipped the bag closed and followed me out of the van.

"Get down, will you?" Quentin whispered, tugging Trent to crouch on the pavement with us. Trent looked confused, but at least he was quiet.

"This way." I crawled to the front of the van. When we reached the open space—we'd have to run from the van, across the road to the brush on the other side of the sheriff's car —I looked over my shoulder. Dr. Ames was turned away from us, talking again with the DEA officer near the crates. "Ready?"

Quentin nodded. "I got him." He grabbed Trent's arm. "We're partners, okay?"

Trent frowned. "I generally prefer to work alone."

"Don't let go of him." I scanned the roadside; there was a break in the trees—not a trail but enough space for us to get through. "There." I pointed. "Head that way, and then we'll . . ." What were we going to do? How would we find our way to Molly when we didn't even know where we were or where she was? "Then we'll find a place to hide. Come on!"

I ran.

My sneakers pounded the hot pavement, and smoky air burned my throat. I didn't look back, but I heard footsteps thumping behind me. I prayed none of them belonged to Dr. Ames.

I kept running, through the break in the trees. Sharp branches scratched my cheeks, and blood dripped down my face.

Had we all gotten away? Were they chasing us? I couldn't slow down to find out.

I pushed the brush aside, floundering, tripping, gasping for breath. I don't know how long I ran, how far—but finally, I couldn't breathe anymore. I was choking on the smoke. My head was pounding, my ankle throbbing from where I'd tripped over a rock, and I knew I was slowing down.

That's when a hand closed on my arm and pulled me to the ground.

24

IT WAS SARAH.

"Stop! I can't . . . I have to . . ." She couldn't catch her breath, and I couldn't catch mine. I clung to her.

We heard branches cracking toward us, but there was nowhere to hide, and we couldn't run anymore, so we waited.

"Ben!" Sarah cried as he pushed through the trees and sank to the ground next to us.

But instead of looking relieved, Ben looked upset, anguished. He buried his head in his hands. "I screwed everything up! I should have just let you go. Now I'll never get back."

I reached for his arm. "Yes, you will. We're all going to get back home." I was trying to reassure myself, too.

Ben swatted my hand away. "I don't want to go home!"

"What?" He wasn't making sense. I waited until he looked up at me. "Listen to me, Ben. I know you want to go home, and you're going to make it. We're going to find Molly, and she'll help us. She will."

Ben shook his head as if I didn't understand at all. Tears spilled down his face.

"Where are Quentin and Trent?" Sarah stood up, and I did, too. Even if they weren't coming, we had to keep moving.

Ben swiped at his muddy, tear-stained face with his sleeve. "They were behind me, but I think they turned off a different way."

"Was anybody chasing you?" I held my breath.

"I don't think so." Ben bit his lip.

I brushed myself off and reached down for his hand. "We have to go." He took it, then winced as if I'd hurt him, and let go and got up by himself. "We have to find Quentin and Trent." This was all falling apart already. "Then we can—"

"We should go back," Ben said.

"Back?" Sarah stepped toward him as if she might shove him to the ground. "Are you out of your mind?"

"Wait!" I grabbed Sarah's arm. "He's right . . . we'd know by now if Dr. Ames was chasing us. He must have given up. Maybe we can follow the road back to the dock. It's our best chance of finding Quentin and Trent, and then when we get to the dock, maybe there will be a boat or . . . somehow we'll be able to get to Molly. And if we can't find her, then . . ."

I sounded stupid and too full of hope, even to myself. But I couldn't think about the possibility that I'd never get home to Mom and Dad, to Aunt Beth and Kathleen. To our houseboat and the sea lions and the bay. And back to school. I wanted another chance at middle school, a chance to decide who I wanted to be there, instead of following Lucy all the time.

I started walking. "Come on. We'll backtrack until we hear traffic. Then we can find a place to check things out."

"Yeah." Ben nodded, and his voice was stronger. "That sounds good."

It was slow; walking through sawgrass was like trying to swim through an ocean of seaweed. When we hugged the tree line, we stumbled and tripped over roots.

Every time we ventured out from the shade, the noon sun threatened to melt us into the ground. Our bags were still back with the van. We didn't have hats or sunblock or even water, and by the time we started hearing road noises, we were all close to collapsing.

"Stop!" Sarah grabbed my arm. "Listen."

I stood still, the sun hot on my scalp, sweat dripping down my temples, but all I heard was the buzz of the deerflies that had been dogging me the whole walk. I'd already been bitten half a dozen times.

"There . . . listen!" Sarah said again, and this time, I heard voices—quiet voices. Soft and low. It didn't sound like Dr. Ames, but I couldn't be sure.

"I think it's coming from this way," I whispered, and ducked to the right between two spindly pine trees. We took a few steps . . . waited . . . listened . . . heard nothing but flies and rustles of grass when a rare breeze blew. It was never enough to cool our faces. We kept going that way until Sarah stopped me again.

"Over here!" She took off, faster.

"Sarah, wait," I hissed. "What if . . ."

But she'd already run ahead, and I heard the relief in her voice. "Quentin!"

He was huddled next to Trent in the measly shade offered by a thick old tree stump that jutted up from the dry grass. Trent had his electronics spread out on the stump and was working again, muttering something about direct currents. Quentin jumped up as soon as he saw us. He put a finger to his lips. "The road is right over there." He pointed to a thicker clump of brush to our left. Highway noises—motors and trucks braking—came through the trees.

"Are they still there?" I asked.

He shook his head, but his face was grim. "They're gone. I don't know if the police ever caught that Gus guy, but Dr. Ames took off in the van maybe twenty minutes ago. He's all buddy-buddy with the cops now; when they let him go, they *apologized* for the inconvenience."

"So why are you still here?" Sarah asked.

Quentin pointed to Trent, who hovered, tinkering with whatever it was on the tree stump. "He's fixing Dr. Ames's cell phone."

Trent held up a finger. "I must warn you that the conditions out here are not favorable, and I can't promise to have this device functioning anytime soon, given the circumstances. But yes, I am attempting to repair the connection."

"Attempting to repair the connection?" My heart sank. We never had a chance to call our parents and tell them the truth, that we were alive, that we were here and needed help. "What happened?"

Quentin cringed. "Fell out of my pocket onto the road while we were running. I snagged it, but now it won't pick up a signal." He looked down at Trent, working diligently at his stump. "He thinks the antenna inside came loose."

Tears burned my eyes, but I blinked them away. "Which way did they go?"

Quentin tipped his head, confused.

"The DEA guys. And Dr. Ames. Did they head back toward Everglades City?"

"No, they kept on that way." Quentin pointed in the other direction, down the road the sheriff's deputy said was off-limits because of the fires.

I squatted down next to Trent. "How's it going with the phone?"

"Slowly. I believe I'm making progress, though," he murmured, turning it over in his hands.

"How about if we get you back to your lab so you have better tools?"

He nodded briskly and began gathering his wires and batteries. I reached for the phone, but he grabbed it and glared at me.

"Fine," I said. "Don't lose it." I turned to Quentin. "Let's stay hidden but follow the road back toward Everglades City. It's our best chance to find help. We can find Molly, or maybe the National Guard troops that are helping with the fire will be . . ."

Quentin was shaking his head, biting his lip.

"What?"

He took a deep breath and swatted at a deerfly buzzing around his eye. "When I was looking for the phone, I heard them, Cat. I heard them talking to Dr. Ames."

"The National Guard guys?"

He nodded miserably. "They're not going to help us. They've been ordered to track us down."

"But . . ." I couldn't finish the sentence. It didn't make sense. "But that's not . . . Dr. Ames is working with a *terrorist* group, Quentin. How could the whole National Guard be part of that?"

Ben laughed.

"You think this is funny?" Quentin whirled around to face him.

"I think *you're* funny," Ben said, standing his ground. "For someone who's supposed to be the genius of your family, you're pretty slow to figure things out."

Quentin crossed his arms, and his eyes blazed at Ben. "You have it all figured out? You think you know everything because you've been all cozy with Dr. Ames? Go ahead. Explain how the National Guard got tied up with this terrorist group, because we'd love to know. And while you're at it, maybe you can tell us how to get away."

Ben looked at Quentin as if he felt sorry for him. "Well, first of all, we're not going to get away. They're going to find us and take us back." He sounded as if he were looking forward to that. "And second, the National Guard is not working with terrorists."

"Then why are they following orders to track us down?" I blurted. "Quentin just said—"

"Oh, they're looking for us. But they're not working for terrorists, and neither is Dr. Ames. This project is—"

"Are you stupid?" Quentin threw his hands up in the air. "With everything we've seen—the files and the DNA codes and . . . and Trent—how can you still say that they're not trying to change us into these scientists?"

"I'm not saying that at all." Ben smiled so calmly, it made me shiver, even as sweat matted my hair to my face. "That's exactly what they're doing—creating a team of new-world thinkers to tackle our nation's greatest challenge."

Sarah started toward him. "But you just said—"

Ben held up his hands. "I said they weren't working for terrorists. And they're not. This whole thing is a top-secret, elite forces project of the United States government."

25

"YOU'RE TELLING US THAT OUR own government would . . ." Quentin stared at Ben, and his words trailed off as if he just couldn't believe it.

Neither could I. "*What?*" I'd heard Ben fine; his voice was loud and clear, strong and sure. But he *had* to be wrong. "Ben, if that's true, then—"

"No." Sarah pushed past us and started walking deeper into the brush. "That's garbage, and I don't know what's really going on, but no matter what, we have to get out of here."

"Do whatever you want," Ben called, following her through the trees, "but it's true."

"No, it's not!" Sarah whirled around. "It's a lie, Ben. It's *all* lies! They've been lying to us from the beginning."

"She's right," I said. Sarah was already forging ahead, and the rest of us followed her. Even Ben knew we couldn't stay out here and wait to be found. "Ben . . . what they told you . . . it can't be true. It just can't." It had already been a struggle to accept that Dr. Ames and Dr. Gunther weren't really helping us, that they were working with some terrorist group to change us into geniuses who could work for them.

Now Quentin was telling us the people who were *supposed* to be on our side—even the soldiers—couldn't be trusted. And Ben claimed our own government was doing this to us. I needed them to be wrong. I took a deep breath and tried to calm my voice. "Ben, what exactly did Dr. Ames say?"

"I told you the truth," Ben said, ducking under a tree limb. He wouldn't say any more. "Believe whatever you want."

I wanted to scream. It couldn't be real. "Quentin, when you said the National Guard was searching for us . . . maybe you misunderstood the whole thing. Maybe they were really—"

Quentin stopped so fast I would have run into him if we hadn't been moving so painfully slow through the brush. He whirled around. "Do you think I *want* to believe this? Do you think I feel good about telling you *nobody*'s going to help us? I know what I heard, Cat."

But I couldn't let it go. "*What* did you hear?"

He squeezed his eyes closed, then opened them. "Dr. Ames walked right up to the National Guard truck. Right up to the guy who was driving—he had stripes on his jacket; he was definitely in charge—and Dr. Ames said, 'It's about time. Have you been in touch with Senator Wiley?' And the National Guard guy said, 'We got the order, Dr. Ames. We're to provide you with whatever you need, *sir*.'" Quentin glared at me. "Is that sure enough for you?" He turned and started walking again, with Trent and Ben beside him. I could tell Quentin was furious with Ben, but I could also tell he believed him.

I tried to swallow, but my throat was dry. I nodded, even though he had already turned away. And I followed them.

Sarah tried to stay with me. Her cheeks were blotchy red, and she was starting to stumble.

We kept moving, but no one talked about what we'd do when we got to the dock. What if there wasn't a boat? What if there was? We didn't even know if Molly was still in the swamp.

We couldn't get too close to the road without being seen, so we hiked through the muck and shadows. Tangled roots snatched at our ankles, and it was slow.

The flies made me want to scream. I slapped at one and then another and another, waving the air until I was out of breath.

Sarah looked at me, her eyes empty. Her face was covered in welts; she wasn't even brushing the flies away anymore. "How far do you think we went in that van?"

"Not that far," Quentin said, pausing. He'd been leading the way with Trent, who somehow didn't seem to tire like the rest of us. I wondered if his "treatment" made him stronger as well as smarter. "Maybe we can see a landmark by the road." Quentin started toward the highway sounds, and we followed until he put up a hand. "I'll make sure it's clear."

We crouched in the brush and waited while he pushed through the scrubby trees.

"See anything?" Sarah called.

Quentin didn't answer, but slowly, he backed away from the road. Halfway to us, he started running, and even though it wasn't very far, he was wheezing when he crouched down next to us. "They're stopped . . . there on the road," he said, panting.

"Who? Dr. Ames?" Ben's eyes were wild.

"Maybe. I didn't see him," Quentin said. "But two National Guard trucks are parked on the shoulder, and a bunch of guys with phones are standing around them."

Ben sprang to his feet and took off, scrambling through the high grass, running toward the road.

"Here! Over here!" he screamed. "We're here!"

26

QUENTIN HADN'T PLAYED FOOTBALL SINCE his concussion, but he remembered how to tackle. He leaped into a run, flung himself at Ben's torso, thumped him to the ground, clapped a hand over his mouth, and dragged him back to where Sarah, Trent, and I still crouched, staring.

"What is the matter with you?" Quentin hissed. His eyes were on fire. "If they find us . . ." He looked around wildly, holding his breath, but the only sounds were road traffic. Ben's shouts had apparently been drowned out by truck engines.

Quentin's voice sounded tight enough to explode. "If they'd heard you . . . if they find us, they'll give us right back to Dr. Ames." He glared at Ben. "I can't believe you'd do something so idiotic!"

Ben yanked his arm away from Quentin and started to run again, but this time, three of us latched on to him and pulled him down. Quentin locked his forearm around Ben's neck.

"Don't choke him! He's not thinking straight!" I was afraid

Quentin might hurt Ben; the look on his face was so wild. "He doesn't understand."

Ben's jaw clenched, and sweat shone on his face. "You're wrong," he said. "I do understand." He struggled against Quentin's grasp, but Quentin was bigger. He twisted Ben's arm behind his back. Ben winced, but he kept talking. "You think you're so smart? I only got out of that stupid van with you so I could make sure you didn't get away and let the whole thing fall apart. I've known the truth all day." He leaned forward and spit in the dirt.

"*What* have you known?" I stared at him.

"Everything. I asked Dr. Ames what was going on, right after we found the flight information. He told me the truth because he knew *I* could handle it. He knew I'd do the right thing."

"What?" Sarah gaped.

"What truth?" Quentin's voice was strained, but he kept it under control. We needed Ben to keep talking. "About this whole thing being a government project?"

"That's right." Ben's face was smeared with sweat and dust and blood from his nose, from Quentin's tackle. But his eyes were sharp. And his voice . . . his voice was full of pride. "We are part of an important, highly classified military project. In fact, we *are* the project."

Trucks rumbled on the road—louder than before—and suddenly, Ben flailed out at Quentin again. I jumped up and helped Quentin hold him. We waited while the engines' roars faded and finally gave way to insect hum and frog peeps.

"They're gone." I let go of Ben's arm, and his body went

slack. He sank to the ground, and Quentin let him go. There was nowhere for Ben to run now, no one left for him to call.

Finally, Sarah spoke in a weak voice. "So they really did plan to use us?"

"We're going to be the new Manhattan Project. They've been calling us Team Phoenix." Ben's face glowed. His voice was full of energy, even though he'd walked just as far as we had, through the heat and without water. Was it because he was the only one of us who still believed in something? He wasn't talking in the past tense; he was talking as if this Team Phoenix project was still going to happen, as if he couldn't wait.

It still felt unreal to me. But ideas exploded in my mind. "Team Phoenix?" Sarah and I had seen the phrase in Dr. Gunther's e-mail, but we'd figured it was some sports team in Phoenix, Arizona. Now, I remembered another phoenix, the immortal bird from mythology that Mrs. Rock told us about in English class, the one that bursts into flame at the end of its life and then rises from the ashes, reborn.

"I said I told you the truth. Dr. Ames and Dr. Gunther were never working with terrorists," Ben went on. "They're *fighting* terror. Team Phoenix is going to create new technologies and cures for diseases and weapons. And as soon as we get to the other clinic, they're going to introduce the new genetic material, and we're going to be brilliant. I'm getting Albert Einstein's DNA. Quentin's going to be Oppenheimer." He turned to Sarah. "You're getting DNA from Lise Meitner. She's this amazing scientist who escaped from the Nazis and did calculations that led to the discovery of nuclear fission. Isn't that awesome?"

"No!" Sarah hugged her arms around herself, as if that could keep any of this from happening.

Ben kept going. "And Cat, you're getting Beatrice Shilling's DNA. She was an aeronautical engineer who figured out the technology to let World War Two fighter pilots dive without their planes stalling." He looked at me as if he expected me to cheer, to be thankful that they wanted to make me into someone else. Then he held his arms wide as if they could pull us all together. "We're going to be the dream team that makes America the most powerful nation in the world. Nobody will mess with us." Even though he sat, filthy, in the mud, Ben's eyes were bright. "Dr. Ames and Dr. Gunther are the best in their field, and they were chosen—*we* were chosen—to bring America back to greatness."

"You believe all that?" Quentin's voice rose. "You think you were *chosen* because you're special? You were chosen because you had the crummy luck to get a concussion that made the right part of your brain vulnerable, so you got sent here like the rest of us."

"Ben, think about it," Sarah said. Her voice was sad. "How else could they get subjects for this project? You think people would volunteer to have their personalities wiped out?" She gestured toward Trent and his miniature laboratory-in-the-field. "Look at Trent! And who was Kaylee supposed to be? Marie Curie? She's sick, Ben; she might be *dying*. They *lied* to us. They tricked our parents. And they're lying to you, too."

"They're telling our parents we're dead. What about your family?" As soon as I said it, I remembered. His parents were gone—his mom a long time ago and his dad, more recently, in Afghanistan.

Quentin remembered, too. His voice was softer. "Ben, man . . . I know . . . I know your dad was a hero. But this isn't how he gave his life for his country. He made a choice to serve. He went into it—"

"*I'm* making a choice." Ben's voice was calm but strong. "I want to do this."

"But . . ." I looked at Trent, so lost in the complicated connections of his own brain, he was barely aware that we existed. "But look at him!" I pointed to Trent. He never looked up. "He was somebody's big brother. He used to laugh and make jokes and play basketball, and now he's . . ." Trent's eyes lit up. He reached into his backpack and pulled out a pair of needle-nose pliers. "He's none of those things anymore."

"He's something better." Ben took a deep breath. "And besides, when this is all over, when the project is done, they can reverse everything. They'll reintroduce our old DNA and reload our old memories. *If* we want." He sounded like he couldn't understand why anybody would want that, why anybody would want to be only who they are, and it made my heart hurt. I wanted my old self back, my old life back, so badly I felt like I might break into pieces.

"Dr. Ames told you that?" Quentin said. "He told you they'd change you back if you want, when it's over?"

Ben nodded.

"You believe them? They lied before."

Ben's eyes narrowed. "They lied to *you*. Because they didn't think you were ready to know. They told *me* the truth." He stood, but he didn't try to run again. Instead, he walked slowly to the one gnarled cypress tree that grew up out of the brush and ran his hand down its smooth side. "Dr. Ames knew I'd understand." He looked up at the sky; the sun glowed behind the haze of the fires and humidity. "He knew I'd want to make my dad proud."

"Your dad would never want this!" I ran to him, grabbed his shoulders as if I could shake him into seeing. "He would want you to live a long, good life. As *you*!"

Ben didn't shove me again, or push away my hands. He looked me in the eye. "He'd want me to serve my country. He'd want me to make my own choices. And I want to do this."

"Well, we don't." Quentin stood and brushed his hands together. "You don't get to choose for the rest of us. And we're leaving. We're going back to try and find help. If you want to stay here or run out to the road and wait for the National Guard or whatever, that's—"

"I want to go to the clinic," Ben said. "Dr. Gunther is there, and he can help us get back to—"

"Not us. *You*. Get *you* back." Quentin's eyes were threatening.

"Fine. *Me*."

Trent jerked his head up. "I'm going back as well. I can't continue to make progress under these conditions. I need equipment from the workshop."

"He doesn't know what he's saying." Sarah threw her hands in the air. "He's not even—"

"No," I said. "It's okay." I turned to Quentin and Sarah and whispered. "We need to go back into the swamp to find Molly. After we find her—after we're safe—then Ben can go on to the clinic if he wants. It won't matter. Until then, we keep him with us."

Quentin nodded slowly and turned to Ben. "If you want to go back to the clinic, we need to stay together or we'll never make it. We're going back to the dock, and then we're going to find Molly to get help."

"Fine." Ben smirked.

"Listen to me." Quentin got right in his face. "Once we're safe, you can do whatever you want. If you want to go back, we won't stop you. But we have the right to make our own choices, too. So if we see trucks and you try to run again, I'm going to beat the snot out of you."

Quentin's eyes were like stone. He didn't look anything like the friendly, patient kid I'd met a week ago. He'd never even started Phase Three, but I-CAN had changed him, too.

Ben's jaw twitched as if he might take off running for the National Guard again. We knew we couldn't trust him, but we had to keep going, and we had to take him with us. There was no other choice.

Quentin stared him down, his fists clenched, and finally, Ben nodded. "Fine. Let's go."

27

THERE WAS TOO MUCH TO think about and nothing left to say. We trudged on and on through the brush, stumbling more often, getting up more slowly, until dark clouds moved across the sun.

"Oh, please rain. Please rain." Sarah looked at the sky as if she'd climb up herself to get the rain if it didn't hurry.

Trent looked at her thoughtfully, then jogged over to a shrub and picked some fruit that looked like little plums. "Here. They're edible and have significant water content."

She hesitated. "Are you sure?"

Trent nodded, and Sarah smiled at him. For just a second, he smiled back. He had dimples, and I got a glimpse of the boy she'd told me about. I could imagine him fooling around with his food, laughing in the cafeteria, or cheering at a basketball game. "Thanks," Sarah said, and passed some fruit to the rest of us. "It tastes like a banana only not as sweet."

Trent nodded, and his face went serious again. "It's *Chryso-balanus icaco*. Be mindful that you don't swallow the pit."

She tipped her head and looked at him. "How do *you* know all this stuff?"

He shrugged. "I'm quite familiar with my native flora and fauna." He glanced around, then reached past Sarah to pluck some long, pointy leaves from a shrub. "*Myrica cerifera*, for example, is an excellent insect repellent." He crushed the leaves and held them out to us.

Quentin frowned at the crumbled leaves in his hand, then over at Trent. "Have you spent much time studying the animal and plant life here?"

Trent nodded seriously. "Years." And he started walking again.

Sarah looked at me, bewildered, as she rubbed the leaves on her arms. "He's from *Queens*."

"The file on the computer said Edison spent time in Florida," I whispered, remembering that day in Dr. Gunther's office. "He had an estate in Fort Myers or somewhere. Come on . . . let's catch up."

It was hard to guess how long we walked. Trucks rumbled by on the road—we didn't get close enough to see if they were National Guard—but Ben didn't try to run again. He seemed intent on getting back to the clinic, where he could reconnect with Dr. Gunther and get himself back to Dr. Ames.

Quentin stopped and looked to the west. "I think that was thunder."

"Good." Sarah tipped her head up as soon as the first fat drops plunked down. But the rain never picked up, even though lightning struck not far away, and thunder boomed a second later. The whole swamp shook.

The storm seemed to feed life back into Sarah, even though

not much water made it into our mouths. She started climbing over a fallen tree that crossed our path. "Do you think Molly will have food when we find her? Because those plum things were okay, but I'm—"

"Watch it!" Ben shoved Sarah so hard she flew off the log, into me, and I nearly knocked Quentin into the grass.

"What the—" Quentin began, but stopped. We saw the snake at the same time. It twitched into a tight coil beside the log, right where Sarah would have put her foot down if Ben hadn't pushed her. Its muscles rippled underneath thick, muted bands of copper and black.

"She startled it." Ben took a step back, broke a branch off a nearby tree, and prodded the snake. Its mouth opened wide and glowed white. "Cottonmouth," he said.

The snake struck at the stick, its head darting forward quicker than Sarah would have been able to leap out of the way.

"Oh . . ." Sarah bit her lip, blinking fast. "I almost—oh!" She turned toward Trent and reached for his arm, shaking. He looked down at her hand, and again, just for a second, his eyes flickered with something softer and warmer than genius.

But then he pulled away and shook his head a little, as if he were shaking away a cobweb. "*Agkistrodon piscivorus* is a notoriously aggressive variety of pit viper." He turned to Ben. "You were prudent to forcibly remove her from harm's way."

"Yeah, well . . ." Ben eased the long stick underneath one of the snake's coils, lifted it from the ground, and flung it into the brush off to our left. We watched it twist away into the weeds.

"Uh . . . thanks." Sarah's hands were still shaking.

Ben shrugged. "I saw one with Dr. Ames when we were out walking a few days ago. He said you have to watch for them around here."

I took a deep breath. The smoke seemed stronger, thicker. "Do you smell that? Aren't we heading away from the fires?"

"We were," Quentin said, "but there's lightning all over. Could be a new strike set off another one."

We started walking again. Sarah made us go ahead of her, and we all stepped more carefully, our eyes scanning the ground. Twisty, gnarled roots sent my heart into my throat every few steps. But there were no more snakes. Just more smoke.

"My throat's burning," I said. "Let's get to the road and see where we are."

We pushed through the trees, and cool water drops fell from their leaves, leftovers from the rain shower. I tipped my head up so they'd wash my face.

"Oh, look!" Huge air plants dotted the branches above us, hung with moss like witches' hair. Quentin shook one of the trees, and water rained down.

"Wait, don't do that!" I searched the bottom of a tree for a foothold, someplace to start climbing, and found a low branch. "They're full of water." I flung a leg over the branch and pulled myself up. I paused, waiting for the fear to come. I hadn't been in a tree since my fall, but somehow, my brain let my body keep climbing. Maybe because I needed water so badly. Or maybe because I knew now there were things so much worse than falling.

Slowly, branch by branch so I wouldn't shake the plants dry, I climbed, until I could reach the lowest one. The flower was a brilliant, spiky red. I loosened the plant from its branch, pulled it down, and tipped it to my mouth. The leaves prickled my cheeks, but I didn't care. The water was warm and wet and perfect. "Come up!" I called. "But be careful not to shake everything."

They all climbed. Trent even abandoned his bag of electronics so he could scramble up into the wet leaves. We drank from every plant that held water—dozens of them—and I sighed and closed my eyes, leaning against a branch, until the sound of a truck engine found its way through the trees.

"The road must be near," Quentin called up. I was a few branches higher. "Can you see anything?"

I couldn't. But there was another branch above mine. Slowly, I stood, grabbed it with both hands, and pulled myself up. The bark had scraped my palms so one was bleeding, but what I saw made up for that.

"The road's right there," I said, "and so is the driveway that goes down to the docks."

Maybe I just felt better because I'd finally had something to drink, but the sight of that gravelly driveway filled me with hope. Still, I had no idea what we'd find when we got down to the water.

28

WE HID IN THE TREES until all the car sounds faded away, until we were sure we could cross the road unseen, and then we ran. It felt so good to fly across flat asphalt with nothing tripping me or scratching at my legs, no shadows that coiled into snakes with bright, gaping mouths.

On the other side of the road, we stopped running, but we walked on the open driveway—not in the brush. If a vehicle turned, we'd hear tires on the gravel long before anyone could see us, and we could dive for cover.

Ben hadn't said anything else about Dr. Ames or the clinic's plan. Somehow, since he pushed Sarah away from the snake, he felt like one of us again. It was better that way, better for us not to talk about what might happen after we found Molly—*if* we found her.

"Do you remember if there was a building or anything down here?" Quentin said. "Maybe there's a phone."

"I don't think so." I'd looked around when I was stalling, not wanting to get in that van. "There might have been bathrooms, but that's about it."

"What if there's somebody here?" Sarah whispered. We were getting closer. "What if those drug guys are back?"

"I don't know." Quentin slowed a little.

We'd spent so much of our energy and hope getting back here that I hadn't let my brain fast-forward past this moment. Sarah had a point. What if those guys *were* at the dock? What if Dr. Ames was waiting for us?

And what if there was no one at all? No help. No boats. The river was full of snakes and alligators, and we were exhausted. There was no way we could swim all the way to . . . Where were we even going?

We'd pinned all our hopes on Molly, and we had no idea where she was.

"Let's check around this bend before we go ahead," Quentin said, pulling us close to the trees. "The parking lot is up here."

But before we'd taken five steps, gravel crunched behind us—a car or truck speeding down to the lot. Quentin jumped into the bushes and pulled Trent in after him. Ben, Sarah, and I crouched in the high grass as a rusted blue pickup barreled down the driveway, kicking up stones and splashing mud. The back was stacked with crates.

I caught a glimpse of the driver's baseball hat. "It's that Gus guy from the van!" I whispered. "He must have gotten away from the police."

Quentin hurried along the edge of the road. "We need to see what he's doing."

We heard the truck engine die. A door slammed. Deep voices. "What the devil happened to you? And where's the van?"

"That quick fifty bucks you promised led me right into a roadblock. Feds."

Staying low, we crept around a bend and hid behind the porta potties at the edge of the lot. The sewage-and-chemical smell would have made me puke if I'd eaten. Instead, it made my stomach twist.

The pickup was parked at the dock, next to an airboat.

"That's the guy who took us from the clinic!" Quentin hissed.

The airboat driver with the vine tattoo was perched on his seat, leaning back, swigging down a Gatorade.

Gus opened the truck's tailgate and tugged on one of the crates. It scraped against the metal truck bed, then thunked as he loaded it onto the airboat.

"Help me with this, will ya, Eugene?"

"Eugene?" Sarah mouthed. It would have been funny under different circumstances; he didn't look like a Eugene. Somehow, Eugenes weren't supposed to have scars and tattoos.

Eugene lifted a crate, then eyed the others left in the truck. "Where's the rest?"

"I told you. Feds had a roadblock. They got two prime batches. Almost took me with 'em, no thanks to you." He lifted a crate and hauled it onto the boat.

The airboat sat lower and lower in the water as the crates piled up.

"Where do you think they're taking it?" Quentin whispered.

"Someplace to hide it." I didn't know where, but I could guess.

Back into the swamp, to one of those run-down shacks in the mangrove islands. There was only one path into the swamp from here—the one that led back to the clinic. Where we needed to go. It sounded crazy, but I knew their airboat might be our only chance to get there. "We have to go with them."

"What?" Sarah grabbed my arm as if she thought I might take off running like Ben.

But Ben was staying close to Quentin. He looked afraid of these guys, even though they'd been working for Dr. Ames.

"Not now," I said, slipping my arm out of Sarah's grasp. "Not with them right there, but . . ." But what? I peered around the edge of the porta potty to get a better look at the boat. An airboat wasn't like the big yachts people took out on the bay at home. There was no cabin, no galley, no place to hide. The deck was wide open except for those crates.

I motioned Quentin, Ben, and Sarah closer. Trent was pressing buttons on the cell phone he'd been trying to fix. "We need to get on that boat," I whispered. "We can hide between crates—if we push a couple of them forward, it'll make sort of a cave in the middle of the pile."

"How? They're right there," Quentin said.

"I guess . . . We can wait until they start it up. It's so loud, and if they're both in back at the control panels, the piled-up crates should block their view."

"That'll never work," Quentin said. "You saw how the boat sat lower in the water every time they loaded a crate. They're going to notice if five more people jump on board; they'll feel it. And even if they don't, even if we get on the boat, then . . ."

Sarah finished, her eyes wide. "Then we're stuck on a boat full of drugs and . . . and bad guys."

"Listen!" An engine hummed far away. I tensed my muscles, ready to jump back into the trees if I heard tires on gravel. Nothing came down the driveway, but the sound grew louder.

"Look!" Quentin pointed to the sky, where an army-green helicopter was approaching. Were they searching for us?

My eyes darted to the dock. Gus and Eugene were walking away from us, carrying crates to the boat. "Quick! They won't be able to see us yet. Get into the trees!" I pulled Trent to his feet and gave him a push in the direction of the brush, hoping there were no snakes. Sarah, Quentin, and Ben tumbled in after us. Quentin kept a firm grip on Ben's arm; he still wasn't taking any chances.

The helicopter whirred louder and louder, until the woods vibrated, until I felt like its blades were spinning inside me. It hovered over the water. Gus and Eugene froze—but then it lifted higher and roared away.

"They're looking for us," Quentin whispered. "They must be." He peered out of the trees, toward the boat.

"If we can get on that boat," I whispered, "and they go to one of those mangrove islands, then whenever they start unloading, we can run." It sounded impossible, but we needed help. And help was somewhere in there, with Molly. In the swamp.

Ben shook his head. "I'm not getting on that boat," he said. "You can go ahead, but I'm staying here. It's my choice—you agreed. I'm going back to the road."

He stepped toward the parking lot, but Quentin lunged for him, pulling him into the weeds. Ben pushed at Quentin, swinging his fists, but Quentin was a lot bigger.

"Shut up or I'm going to pound you!" Quentin growled. He looked toward the dock, but the two men were back to loading crates. The scrapes and thuds of wood on metal must have kept them from hearing the scuffle in the trees. "You listen." Quentin held a tight hand over Ben's mouth. "You can make your own choice later. Go with them. I don't care. But you're not doing it until the rest of us get away. We're not letting you choose for us."

Ben's eyes were still full of fire, but he stopped struggling.

Quentin tightened his grip. "We're getting on that boat as soon as they start the engine. You're coming with us, and you're going to keep your mouth shut or we'll tell those two thugs that *you* were the one who tipped off the police up there." He glared until finally, Ben nodded weakly. Quentin let go of his mouth, and Ben took a deep, gaping breath.

I stared at Quentin. He'd changed so much. He wasn't thinking about his concussion or math or science scores or college anymore, I could tell. He only wanted us to survive. With his clenched jaw, his focused eyes, he was going to do it. Survive. *Live.* No matter what it took.

And so was I.

I stepped to his side. Sarah stood next to me, and her hand closed, tight, around mine.

When the helicopter left, Gus and Eugene went back to work, and they were fast. By the time we crept back behind the porta potty, where we could see them again, Gus was hoisting the last crate onto the heap. The boxes were piled three high and took up the whole back of the boat, between the seats.

"When they start the propeller fan, as soon as they're turned away from us, we run," I whispered.

"That's it." Gus lifted his T-shirt and pulled it up to wipe his forehead. "I'm taking the truck up to the road. Billy's coming by to get it so it's not sitting around. He'll shove it in the back of Rocko's barn. You gonna wait here?"

Eugene polished off the last of his Gatorade. "Yeah. I gotta use the can. Hurry up." He started for the porta potty.

We ducked back, squeezed together, and pressed our bodies as close as we could to the hot plastic wall.

The truck door slammed, and gravel crunched as it pulled away.

Eugene's footsteps came closer.

I looked at Quentin, then tipped my head toward the boat. This was a better opportunity than we thought we'd have. We'd need to be fast.

The porta potty shook as Eugene pulled the door shut.

The second it latched, we half walked, half ran for the boat, trying to keep our steps quiet.

"Here!" I whispered, climbing onto the boat. "Help me move these." I squatted, my back against one of the crates, and pushed with my legs. It slid to the side, but the crates behind it were packed together tight.

"Pull—quick!" Quentin grabbed one corner of the next crate, and Sarah grabbed the other, wiggling it to the side to make space between them.

"I hope that guy takes his time," Sarah whispered, stealing a glance at the porta potty. The door was still closed. She reached for the next crate but couldn't move it by herself. There was space between the crates but not enough for all of us.

Ben's eyes darted toward the parking lot—it wouldn't be empty for long—and he started pushing, too. He must have hated the idea of getting caught by Gus and Eugene more than he hated us. "In here!" He shoved Trent down into the cramped space between the crates. Quentin went next, then Sarah, then me.

"Push in! He's coming!" Ben crouched low and folded himself into the tiny space, squeezing me even closer to Sarah. I could feel her heart thumping, her breath, fast and shallow.

"Shhh!"

Ben pulled a crate in front of the opening so we couldn't see out—and couldn't be seen unless someone climbed on top of the crates and peered down at us. I prayed no one would.

The boat dipped in the water—Eugene must have stepped on board. There was the fizz of a can opening—then a pause—and a belch.

"Hurry up, man!"

Running footsteps. The boat dipped again. Gus was back.

Then the engine started, and the roar of the fan drowned out whatever else they might have said—about where they were going, where *we* were going. All I could hear was the thumping roar of wind in my ears as we sped into the swamp.

29

THE RAIN HAD BEEN THREATENING, flirting with us all afternoon. And now it came for real.

A storm surged over the swamp with booms that rattled my heart, even over the roar of the airboat. Thunder shook the sky, and the islands flickered lightning-green. With every flash, my heart raced faster.

What had seemed like our only hope back at the dock felt impossibly dangerous now. Mom would die if she knew I was on a boat with drug dealers. She always told me never, ever get in a car with someone you don't know, no matter what. She said if I ever got lost or needed help I should find another mom. Some lady with kids would always help.

My stomach lurched. There had to be a thousand moms back in Everglades City. Why hadn't we gone there and found one of them instead of sneaking on this boat with these sweaty men and their drugs?

But we'd been so scared, so tired, so thirsty and confused that we chose this. What now?

What if they decided to turn back and unload the boat at the dock? Could they possibly keep going in this storm? Even if they did, how would we find our way to Molly? We had to find her; she was our only hope.

I tried to count the bends in the river.

A lurch to the right, rough wood against my cheek. Another turn, another curve. I'd taken medicine before we left the clinic, but I could feel its effects slipping away. A dull ache threatened behind my eyes, but I pushed it away and tried to focus.

Were we near the crab traps or the bank where the little alligator had been sunning itself? Were we anywhere near One-Eyed Lou?

It was impossible to tell. All I could see from our penned-in space was a crooked rectangle of angry clouds and pouring rain.

Finally—I don't know how long it was, maybe twenty or thirty minutes—the rain let up. And then we slowed down, and the engine quieted.

"Pull 'er up!" one of the men shouted, and the boat thumped against shore. I fell forward into Ben. He caught my shoulder, then pushed the crate in front of him, slowly, the slightest bit, until a sliver of hazy light came through. He pressed his face to the crack, and I waited.

"Can you see anything?"

"They're tying up to a tree. We're on one of those islands," he whispered.

"Start unloading," one of the men said. "I'm gonna climb up and see if I can get a signal and call Rocko. After we get this stuff stashed, we'll have him meet us with the truck."

There were footsteps—then nothing—and then the crate over my head to the right scraped across the one beneath it.

I sucked in my breath and froze.

I heard a grunt and dared to look up.

Thick hands were wrapped around the side of the crate.

Don't let him look down. Don't let him look down.

Another grunt. The crate slid off the pile. The boat tipped as Gus—I could see him from the back now—wobbled under the weight of his load and stepped gingerly off the boat into the shallow water. He cursed, rested the crate on a log for a few seconds while he swiped at his dripping face with a sleeve, then picked it up again and started up a muddy path.

Nothing was hiding us anymore.

"We have to go. Hurry!" I pushed Ben toward the crate that blocked our way off the boat. Who knew how long they'd be gone? They'd have to get the crates up out of the water, but they wouldn't be able to haul them too far. "Push!"

Ben pushed at the crate with his feet, and it scraped across the boat's deck. "Come on." He pulled my hand and steadied me. My legs were cramped, my knees shaky. Quentin and Sarah and Trent climbed out behind me.

"Over here!" I jumped down and sloshed through shallow water to the front of the boat. There was no trail through the trees, but we'd be out of the way, at least partially hidden by the airboat, when Gus and Eugene came back for the rest of the crates.

"Climb up and over." I grabbed a higher mangrove branch and pulled myself up through the leaves, my feet scrambling for lower branches, anything to keep me moving.

We hadn't gone far—the thick tangle of branches slowed us down—when we heard the men slipping back down the muddy trail to the boat. We froze, half hanging over tree limbs, tangled in branches, but out of sight, and we listened.

"Think the stuff'll be safe here? Camp on the other side's better hidden, farther in the brush."

Two crates scraped against one another.

"Nah. That old lady's always hanging around the other one."

My heart jumped. Was Sawgrass Molly nearby?

"So what? She ain't nothin'."

"Saw that dang reporter around there last week, too," the first man said. "This place is better."

Their mud-sloshing footsteps faded up the trail.

"Did you hear that?" I whispered when the men were gone. "We need to get to that other camp. Come on!"

We climbed through mangroves until the voices and grunts and moving sounds faded. Finally, water glimmered on the other side. "The other camp must be over here," I said.

"Look!" Quentin stumbled through the trees, breaking branches as he pushed toward shore, pointing to an airboat pulled up on a mess of rotten logs. "That's Molly's, isn't it?"

We rushed up to it. Molly's bag, with her binoculars, her water, and her knife, was tucked under the seat.

Molly was on the island—on *this* island.

"She's here!" I almost sang the words. Molly was here, and she had her boat, and she could take us . . . wherever she was going to take us before, where she promised we'd be safe while she told somebody what was going on, while she found help.

I imagined Molly's weathered smile and her strong arms, and then, for the first time in forever, I pictured my mom. I'd been afraid to even remember her face, her smell, because remembering would mean admitting I might never see her again for real. I started back up onto shore. My headache was building, but soon, it wouldn't matter anymore. "Let's go . . . she's probably—"

"Shhh!" Quentin grabbed my arm. A motor hum blended with the insect buzz and grew louder. "It's those guys! They must have finished with the crates and come around!" We should have heard them start up the boat—it wasn't that far away—but we didn't. "Over here!" We climbed back into the thick brush, and the five of us huddled together again, waiting.

The roar grew louder. But Gus and Eugene were leaving—they had to be—and then we'd find Molly and she'd take us in the airboat, away from all this.

But when the airboat turned the bend, my breath caught in my throat.

It wasn't Gus and Eugene.

It was Dr. Ames. He steered the airboat slowly, purposefully, close to shore, peering into the trees. He hadn't given up on finding us. If anything, he looked like he was prepared to check every island.

"He's got binoculars," I whispered. He lifted them and scoured the shore across the river.

Quentin sucked in his breath. "He's got a gun." His mouth trembled as he spoke. "On his belt. That holster is the kind my dad and the other officers carry."

Dr. Ames reached down, rested his hand on the black case attached to his belt, then lifted the binoculars again.

"Don't move. Nobody move," said Quentin. He didn't bother whispering. We couldn't be heard over the airboat's roaring fan.

But we could be seen if someone looked carefully enough.

Slowly, carefully, Dr. Ames turned his boat away from the empty island. Toward us.

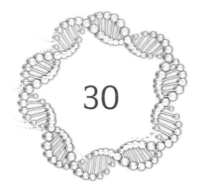

30

"WE CAN'T STAY HERE. WE'LL have to get up into the trees more when he's not looking." Quentin's eyes rested on Ben.

Ben.

I was so focused on watching Dr. Ames that I forgot about Ben. All he had to do was jump out of the brush and wave, and he'd have what he wanted. He'd be back with Dr. Ames. He'd be able to give himself up for the project.

But Ben didn't shout or jump out of the trees.

He didn't move.

Had he changed his mind?

Or was it because of us? I couldn't stop thinking about the way Ben reacted to keep Sarah safe from that cottonmouth. Ben may have been intent on going back to Dr. Ames, but maybe we still mattered to him, too.

"Quentin's right," I said. "We have to go." I looked at Ben and waited until he met my eyes. "Will you come?"

It was barely a nod, but I saw it, and that was enough. "Wait until he looks away." I held my breath and watched the boat drifting, turning in the breeze. I watched Dr. Ames, his thin fingers wrapped around the binoculars.

I hated him.

It was all I could do not to scream, to flail out into the water and pummel him with my fists. All of a sudden, I understood Quentin's fury at Ben earlier. I wanted to go home, to burst out of the trees and run.

But I needed to be still. To wait. And then . . .

"I think he's got the boat stuck," Quentin said.

"He doesn't appear to be following correct operational procedures for that type of vessel," Trent said, frowning. "Perhaps I should go assist him by explaining the proper—"

"No!" Sarah grabbed Trent's arm. "I mean . . . stay with us, please. So we can get you back to the workshop to get your materials."

He looked at her, and I could almost see the old Trent, fighting to surface, to remember they'd been friends and maybe more. But then he simply shrugged. "All right. I'll stay."

"Thanks." Sarah kept her hand on his arm, and Trent didn't pull away. He watched with the rest of us as Dr. Ames put the binoculars behind him on the seat and revved the airboat's engine, trying to get the boat to turn. But he was no Molly, and the airboat pushed deeper into the mud.

"He's looking away. Go!" I pushed Sarah ahead of me, and Quentin pulled Trent along with him. They scrambled over the branches.

I looked back. Dr. Ames was still struggling with the boat's throttle. We had time. I glanced at Ben. He was watching Dr. Ames with a look I never expected. What was it? A mix of sad and hurt and . . . something else. It reminded me of the look I saw on Mom's face when she left the clinic, when she said good-bye. "Come on," I said.

But Ben didn't move.

I wanted to run. I wanted to get away. But if I left Ben behind, Dr. Ames would find us all.

The airboat lurched forward and started to turn our way.

"Ben . . ." I couldn't make him move. I knew that. And Quentin was gone, halfway up the island. "Please. Come with us to find Molly. And then . . . then you can choose."

He looked at the airboat once more, then at me. His face looked as if something were breaking inside him, but he moved. He scrambled up into the trees and reached down to help me up, too. Quentin and Sarah and Trent were up ahead, huddled deep under branches, hidden so well we wouldn't have seen them if Quentin hadn't called to us. When Ben and I found them, we climbed into the nest of leaves and tangled vines, too, and waited.

The airboat engine roared, back and forth, for what felt like hours.

Another military helicopter hovered overhead.

"They're going to see us." Sarah's voice quivered, and she started to cry.

"Shhh! Stop it!" I knew they couldn't hear her—not over the boat's giant fan and the helicopter's whirring blades—but I needed her to stop. I didn't want to hear the truth: we couldn't hide forever.

Hot tears rolled down my face. Muddy streaks marked Quentin's cheeks, too.

Ben didn't cry. His eyes looked empty.

Trent was snapping tiny twigs off the tree, arranging them in some elaborate pattern in the mud. He looked up and saw me watching. "Based on our previous travels, I've constructed an approximate map of the surrounding area, and according to my calculations, once we return to the airboat to depart, we will arrive back at the workshop in eleven to twelve minutes, traveling at a brisk but prudent speed."

"Great. That's great." I wanted to reach into his little map of sticks and knock them out of those tidy lines, fling them in Trent's face. But none of this was his fault. I sighed and watched him move even more twigs carefully into place.

Sarah's sobs faded to a quiet sniffle, and the sky bled from hazy blue-gray to deep, sunset, smoke-stained red. Finally, the helicopters flew away like tired dragonflies, and the airboat's roar died out, too.

I climbed out of the brush and almost collapsed; my legs were so cramped, and I was so weak from not drinking or eating. But I saw what I needed to see.

"He's leaving." Dr. Ames was driving his airboat away, around the bend in the river that led back to the clinic. Away from us.

For now.

31

WE KNEW DR. AMES HADN'T given up. "He'll be back in the morning. Come on." Quentin pointed to an overgrown path that led into the twilight trees. It felt like we'd looped in a thousand circles already, but we followed the trail to a ramshackle hut. Its windows were thick with grime and dust, and it looked like it might collapse any minute. But there were footprints in the mud around the door.

"This isn't the cabin where we found her before," I said, "and those tracks are too big to be Molly's. Plus there are two sets. This must be where those guys hid the drugs."

I reached for the door, but Ben grabbed my hand. "What if they're in there?"

"They wouldn't stick around. They were unloading and that Rocko guy was picking them up somewhere, remember?" I reached for the handle, and the door pushed open with a creak.

The whole building was smaller than Mom and Dad's bathroom, and the dull light that made it through the grimy windows made it feel even more claustrophobic. The crates from the boat were stacked along one wall. Next to the door was a cardboard box full of bottled water.

"Jackpot!" Sarah rushed over and tossed one to each of us.

I guzzled mine so fast my stomach hurt. It helped, but it wasn't what we needed most. We needed Molly.

"They said there was another camp, not far away. That one must be Molly's," I said. We shoved more water bottles into our pockets and pulled the door closed.

"Here's the trail." Sarah pointed between two trees at the back of the building, and we hurried down the overgrown path. With the last light seeping away, mosquitoes rose from the bushes in clouds. I brushed at my neck and brought down a handful.

"How far is it?" Sarah stepped over a log, then ducked under a low-hanging branch, and screamed bloody murder.

A yellowish snake had dropped from the branch onto her shoulder. She whipped her arm around and flung it into the trees.

I rushed to her side. "Did it bite you?"

"No." Her face was still twisted in horror. "But it was *on* me. What if it was another cottonmouth? I can't believe—"

"Definitely not *Agkistrodon piscivorus*," Trent said from over in the trees, where he was watching the snake slither into the shadows. "Its coloration and arboreal nature would suggest *Elaphe obsoleta rossalleni*, the Everglades rat snake. And while it may have alarmed you," he told Sarah, "I can assure you that it's a nonvenomous species and is completely harmless."

"Yeah . . . except when it gives you a heart attack." She brushed her shoulder as if she could still feel it there. "What *is* it with me and snakes? Somebody else go first."

Quentin stepped past her and continued down the trail. It opened into a clearing with another shack, even more run-down than the first.

We paused at the edge of the clearing. The door was partway open, but there were no windows, and inside, it was dark.

"Molly's not here either." My heart threatened to pull the rest of me right down to the ground. I reached for a branch to steady myself, but I didn't feel like going on. I didn't feel like staying on my feet. It would be so easy to lie down and give up.

"Maybe she's asleep," Quentin whispered. "I wish we had a flashlight or—"

As if he had wished it into being, a light glimmered through the brush on the other side of the clearing.

"Get back!"

We scrambled into the dark of the trees and watched the light bob, flickering in and out of shadows as someone approached.

My neck crawled with feasting mosquitoes, but I didn't move.

"I'm telling you, that scream came from up here," Gus or Eugene said. I knew the voice from the parking lot but couldn't tell which thug it belonged to.

They stepped into the clearing and made a wide arc with the flashlight. We were too far back to be seen—the light wasn't that strong—but it traced paths of leaves and grass and, finally, lit the half-open door of the shack.

"This the one where you saw that old lady hanging around?"

"Yeah . . . looks empty now, though."

Their boots shuffled through the weeds as they approached. When they shone the light through the door, I leaned forward, pushing against a horizontal tree branch to see if I could make out anything inside. Suddenly, one of them came stumbling back.

"Holy mother of . . ."

One of them retched.

Someone cursed.

What had they seen in the cabin? I pushed against the creaking branch, leaning closer to the clearing. Closer . . . I couldn't see into the shadows, but if one of them moved aside, then—

Crack! The branch snapped, and I flew forward.

Hands clutched at me—Quentin, Ben, Sarah—pulling me back. I stumbled into them and ended up on the ground.

One of the men cursed again. There were footsteps—urgent, running footsteps. I held my breath.

But they were running away from us, away down the other trail. Scared of a noise in the woods?

I was still on the ground. Warm blood wet my lip where I'd fallen, and I couldn't take a breath without my whole body shaking.

"It's okay," Sarah whispered. "They're gone."

But it wasn't okay. I knew even then.

I scrambled to my feet, pushed my way into the clearing, and reached for the flashlight they'd dropped. It lit up the grass, light-dead-brown.

My hands shook, and the beam made crazy, trembling shadows on the shack's door as I approached and pushed it open.

A scream filled me up inside. I opened my mouth but nothing

came out. My throat burned. I couldn't breathe. I turned away and sank into the weeds.

Quentin pulled the flashlight from my hands, pushed past me, and stared.

He choked out the words I couldn't say aloud.

"It's Molly."

32

I COULDN'T LOOK AGAIN. I'D already seen too much in that glimpse of her body on the floor.

A heap of muddy clothes and blood and flies.

He killed her.

I didn't have to look again to know.

But Quentin went in with the light. He was only gone a few seconds before he came out and told us. "Gunshot."

Molly was dead.

Sawgrass Molly, who wasn't afraid of snakes or alligators or poachers. Who knew every bird in the swamp, the way Aunt Beth knew them in the bay.

Molly, who'd intercepted Dr. Ames in the hangar so he wouldn't catch us snooping, so he'd never know we found Trent and learned the truth about our treatments. Molly, who put herself in danger to keep us out of it. Who promised to help us, promised to come back that night to get us to safety.

Molly. Who never came back to the dock.

And now we knew why.

"We should bury her," Sarah said quietly.

Quentin shook his head. "With what? Are you going to dig a hole with your bare hands?" His words were rough, but his voice was sad.

I understood. It felt like we should do *something*. Say something. A eulogy? A prayer?

But I couldn't go in there again. Not even to say good-bye.

Instead, I stood by the shack and whispered into its weathered wood. "I'm sorry." I knew she was dead because of us.

I slumped against the door. Splinters scratched through my shirt. I was reeling with dizziness. The last of my meds had given in, and my head felt ready to explode. But it didn't matter. Nothing mattered now because she was gone. Without her, we didn't have a chance.

We sank down in the weeds outside the cabin. Because what was there to do? Where was there to go?

We stayed for hours, half-sheltered under the trees. Another thunderstorm came through and rained down on us. The lightning wasn't scary anymore. Other things were so much worse.

Sarah pulled her knees tight to her chest and put her head down in her arms. Quentin sat next to her, staring at the sky. Ben picked up a dead branch and broke it, then broke the halves again, until the pieces were too small to break. He turned one over and over in his fingers and never looked up. Even Trent knew something was horribly wrong. It was hard to tell what he understood, other than how his wires fit together, but now, he sat quietly, hands still, looking off into the night.

We didn't sleep; we just cried, and when we couldn't cry any more, we clung to one another and tried not to think about the body in the shack.

Nobody said it out loud, but we all knew. It was over.

Without Molly, there was no place safe in this swamp, no chance we could get away from Dr. Ames, no one left we could trust.

We might as well have lain down next to her and waited to die.

Somehow, we finally fell asleep, maybe for an hour, maybe two or three. But then sounds in the brush woke us. Raccoons, probably, or possums, but Ben stood up and looked into the dark of the trees. "We should get out of here," he said.

Quentin let out a sharp huff of breath and stared up at him. "And go where?" Then his face twisted with anger. "Do you mean to tell me you'd still run back to Dr. Ames after—"

"What if those guys come back?" Ben blurted. He looked into the trees again, genuinely terrified of the drug runners who had gone screaming away through the brush, and that's when I realized he really didn't know. The rest of us understood as soon as we saw her body, understood we were in more danger than we'd even imagined. But Ben hadn't even let himself consider the possibility that everything he believed was wrong.

"Ben," I said, trying to keep my voice calm. I was afraid if I didn't, Quentin might attack him. "The drug guys were as freaked out as we were. They didn't do this." I let the words hang in the air. "It had to be Dr. Ames."

He winced, as if I'd slapped him. "You don't know that," he

said. "This place is full of dangerous people . . . Molly even said so herself."

"How can you even say that? You—" Quentin sprang to his feet and lunged at Ben, but Sarah caught him by the arm. She was stronger than she looked, and Quentin stumbled.

"Stop!" she said. "He's brainwashed. He doesn't understand!"

"Stop saying that!" Ben railed at her. "You want to know what I understand? I understand that the world is a dangerous place, and my father understood that, but he went away and now he's gone! I understand that life's not fair. I understand that people die and you get thrown in with relatives who don't want you and you suck it up and deal with it." He was sobbing. "And I understand that sometimes you get a chance to make everything matter. And *you* don't understand *that*." He whirled around, spitting words at all of us. "You don't understand what it's like to believe you don't matter anymore . . . and then figure out you do!"

Sarah was crying, still holding on to Quentin's arm, even though his whole body had gone slack. "Ben, you *do* matter. You do. But Dr. Ames—"

"You can't say Dr. Ames did this!" He flung a hand out toward the cabin. "You don't know! You don't!" He crumpled to his knees, clawing at the dry ground and shaking with sobs.

We did know.

And so did he.

I looked at Sarah, swaying like a willow tree next to Quentin, at Trent, staring into the dark. They'd already told our parents we were dead. Kaylee's, too. Was she back at the clinic? Was she still alive?

I looked from the cabin with Molly inside, on the floor, to Ben, in pieces on the ground. Dr. Ames had destroyed both of them.

The tangled mess inside me—feelings twisted tighter than mangrove roots—started to churn. I took a deep breath, and the smoke burned my airways, but I held it in until I thought I'd burst, until everything inside untangled, and the place where that knot had been filled with anger.

And a promise: Dr. Ames wasn't going to destroy me.

"We need to go," I said, echoing Ben's words. We could do this. Sleep had pushed my headache back into the shadows, and I fought to keep it there.

Quentin turned to me, not angry this time. Bewildered. "Where?"

"To the clinic." The words spilled out from a place I didn't know was alive anymore, a place where I still believed I might get home. But it couldn't just be me; it had to be all of us. I was through letting down people who needed me. "We have to get Kaylee, and then . . . then . . ." I didn't know what then. We needed somebody like Molly. Someone good, somebody who would help kids in trouble, who would keep us safe until the truth came out about Dr. Ames.

I thought about my mom. I couldn't even imagine what she was going through—the phone call she got—but I didn't think about that. I pictured her smile, her healing hopes for me when we were having lunch at that place with the tiny scuttling crabs. What would she do if a bunch of scared kids showed up on our dock at home? She'd help. She'd keep them safe. She'd make sure.

The world was full of moms. Full of Mollys. It had to be. We had to find another one. And I knew where we could start.

33

"THE AIRBOAT'S STILL HERE!"

The flashlight reflected off the aluminum of Molly's boat as we scrambled through the trees. We sloshed through the water and climbed onto the deck.

"She left her bag here." Sarah started to reach for it but stopped. "Should we . . . ?"

Quentin reached past her, picked up the bag, and started pawing through it. "If there's anything here we can use, Molly would want us to have it." He pulled out a half-full water bottle, a crumpled baseball hat, a flashlight that actually worked, a cell phone—dead—and a couple of protein bars.

A small white business card caught the light as it fluttered to the boat's deck. I picked it up and shined the light on it. BRADY KENYON, *Miami Herald*. The name was familiar, but before I could figure out why, Quentin dropped the empty bag to the floor. "That's it." He frowned at the airboat controls. "I guess she didn't carry around the operating manual anymore."

I shoved the damp card in my pocket and looked around the boat. "There are paddles under the railing." But we needed to move faster than that. We had to get the fan started.

I held the flashlight while Quentin fumbled with the ignition switch and turned the key, but the fan sat silent. "Come *on!*" He smacked the control panel with the palm of his hand, turned, and almost crashed into Trent, who was peering over his shoulder.

Quentin's eyes lit up. "Hey! You were reading that manual when we were on Eugene's airboat. You know how to run this thing?"

Trent tipped his head, looked at the control panel, and smiled as he stepped up to the driver's seat of the airboat and flicked the ignition switch.

"That's what I tried," Quentin said.

"You have to let the fuel pump build up, then press the accelerator twice before you start the engine," Trent said, as if he'd been running airboats all his life instead of simply breezing through a manual. But I guess Trent remembered things now. Like how to pump the accelerator and turn the key and make the huge propeller fan roar to life.

"Yes!" Quentin held up his hand for a high five, but Trent only glanced at his palm and turned back to the controls.

"You know how to steer and everything?" Quentin asked.

Trent nodded and maneuvered the boat away from the mangrove island.

"We need to go . . ." Quentin looked down the river. A smoky haze still hung in the air, but the rain clouds had cleared, and a fuzzy full moon glowed through the fog.

"This way." I pointed to our left. I recognized the clearing where we'd seen One-Eyed Lou and her babies.

I shined the light up on the bank and saw a pair of glowing red-orange eyes. "There!" Lou was guarding the nest, her babies sprawled on her back. Trent accelerated.

"No, slow down," I said. "Don't scare her." The alligator shifted but stayed on the nest as we drifted past. I wondered if, somehow, she knew we were friends of Molly.

"Slow down. It's right up here, isn't it?" Quentin peered over the front of the boat as the river opened up. "It looks like . . ." He let out a sharp breath. "He's here."

Dr. Ames's airboat was at the dock, lit by the exterior clinic lights.

"He's not at the dock." And all the clinic windows were dark except the one second from the end of the hall—Dr. Ames's office. "If Kaylee's still here"—I didn't let myself stop to think about what might have happened—"then she'll be in her room. If he stays in his office . . ."

"If he's even *in* the office," Quentin said.

"If he's there, we can get Kaylee out the door at the other end of the building."

We pulled the boat up to the dock, and Trent tied the lines in perfect knots. He started up the hill, toward the old airplane hangar.

"Hey, wait!" Quentin called.

"Shh!" I watched him, breaking into a run toward his work-shop. No wonder he'd been so happy to get us here. "Let him go. We'll get him after we have Kaylee on the boat."

The sky was turning from midnight to a not-so-dark dusty blue as we ran to the clinic.

"Anybody know which room is hers?" Quentin asked.

I peered into a window. There were hockey posters on the walls. "This one is yours, Sarah."

She rose on her tiptoes and looked in her own window. "I can't believe . . . ," she started, but shook her head.

I understood.

How could all this be happening to us? How could it be real?

I looked in the next window, and a girl with long black hair lay in the bed, her face turned toward the window, her eyes half-open. When she saw me, they opened wide.

I raised a quick finger to my mouth. *Quiet! Stay quiet!*

She nodded slowly, then sat up in bed, wincing, and pushed herself to her feet. She looked over her shoulder at the door behind her, limped awkwardly to the window, and reached up with her left hand to open it. She wasn't strong enough. Her right hand hung limp at her side.

I reached up; the window opened easily, and she leaned heavily on the sill but didn't speak.

"Kaylee?" I asked.

Her eyes flashed at the mention of her name, and she nodded. One side of her mouth lifted—half a smile. But she didn't speak. I didn't know if she could.

"Listen." I looked around. The sky was lightening to a yellow-blue-pink, but the wet grass was still quiet. "You have to come with us. I know you're sick, and I know they told you your parents are coming, but they're not. They lied, and really . . ." I didn't know where to start.

"You're in danger," Sarah said from behind me. She stepped up to the window. "They're doing . . . they're doing bad things to us."

Kaylee's face filled with panic.

"It's okay." It wasn't. But she had to come with us. It was the only way she might survive. "We have a boat. We're going to find someone to help."

She blinked fast; scared tears rolled down her cheeks.

Quentin stepped forward and held up his broad arms to the window. "Come on. I'll help you down."

She leaned out, but her one arm didn't work—she couldn't even hold on to Quentin—so he ended up dragging her across the window's edge. It must have hurt, but she didn't make a sound.

She was breathing heavy, swaying a little, when she got to the ground.

"Can you walk?" I asked, and she took a tentative step. Her whole right side seemed broken. Sarah and I each put an arm around her, but we kept stumbling.

"Here," Ben said, taking Sarah's place. He was stronger, and together, we made it to the dock.

"Thanks, Ben. We can help her now. You guys should go get Trent."

Ben and Quentin headed for the hangar while Sarah and I eased Kaylee onto the airboat. She sank into a seat and closed her eyes. What could she be thinking? She had to have known something was wrong, horribly wrong, when she got sick and her parents didn't come. A new surge of anger filled my chest.

I looked up at the clinic. The light in Dr. Ames's window was off.

"Sarah, look." I pointed.

Her head jerked to the dark clinic, then toward the hangar, but there was no sign of the boys. "We need to go get them." Her voice shook. "Dr. Ames could come out any minute."

Tears were drying on Kaylee's face, and her breathing had slowed. She was already asleep. To sleep in the middle of this . . . she had to be sicker than any of us had guessed. She needed a doctor—a *real* doctor and a hospital—soon.

"Stay with Kaylee. I'll go." But when I was halfway to the hangar, Quentin and Ben appeared in the door, lugging boxes that spilled over with batteries and wires.

I ran to them. "Hurry up! Why'd you bring all this?"

Quentin's jaw clenched, and he jerked his head back toward Trent, who was lugging a third box. "It was the only way we could get him to come. It's faster than dragging him." They headed for the boat.

I stopped and looked back at the clinic. A new light had come on—the laboratory. What was Dr. Ames doing? Was Dr. Gunther there, too?

"Come on!" Quentin called, looking over his shoulder.

I stared at that one glowing window and remembered the MRI machine, the computers and monitors inside. What had happened to Kaylee in there, to leave her like this? What had they really done to Trent?

Dr. Ames's silhouette passed by the window. He was carrying something big and boxy—a computer?

"Cat! Let's go!" Sarah yelled from the dock. The boys were almost there, but Trent had stopped to pick up some papers that had spilled from his box.

If I ran to the boat now, we might get away. We might find someone to keep us safe, but would anyone ever believe what they'd done? If Dr. Ames took all the computers, all the evidence, it would be as if it never happened at all. We could tell our stories, sure. But they'd say we were scared kids, away from home, maybe still suffering the effects of our injuries. Nobody would ever know the truth.

I took off running.

"*What are you doing?*" Quentin shouted.

"Start the boat! I'm coming!" But I ran the other way. Back to the clinic.

The door at the end was unlocked, the long wood-paneled hallway empty.

I pushed open the first door, to Dr. Gunther's office where we'd first read those files. And my heart stopped.

He was there. Sitting at his desk, his face hidden behind his computer monitor.

I froze.

And waited. He must have heard the door, must have seen it swing open. But he didn't move.

I leaned forward, then took a silent, slow step and looked around the computer monitor.

His eyes were closed, his chest rising and falling with slow breaths.

Asleep.

I backed slowly out the door and pushed it shut but not all the way—the latch might click and wake him.

I should have run, but I couldn't. I couldn't let their awful secret stay buried forever in the swamp. What if they moved some-place else and found new kids for their project?

I waited outside Dr. Ames's door and counted—five, six, seven seconds—there was no sound from inside. I had to do it—do it *now* and run. Were the others still at the dock? How long would they wait for me?

I pushed open the door. The office was empty, the desk clear and dusted. The screen saver of Dr. Ames's laptop cast eerie, twisting blues and greens on the walls.

I stepped up to the desk, closed the laptop screen, and pulled the plug. Someone would be able to power it up later—if we made it.

I hugged the laptop to my chest and turned.

"Catherine?"

Dr. Gunther stood in the doorway.

34

I THOUGHT ABOUT FLYING AT him, shoving his skinny, old body into the doorjamb. Could I push him and get away?

But his eyes were as big as mine. They moved from my face to the laptop in my arms. He turned his head, looked away from me down the long hallway, and stepped back from the door, out of my way.

Was it a trick? Would he let me pass?

I took a hesitant step toward him. Then another.

He stepped back again. There was a sound from down the hallway. He jerked his head and gasped. Then he moved faster than I thought he could, into the room. He pulled the door closed behind him, pushed past me to the window, threw it open, and turned to me with wild, haunted eyes.

"*Run!*"

I didn't ask why, didn't stop to think. I climbed out and stumbled in the flower bed below the window, but I clung to the laptop, and I ran. The boat roared at the dock. Quentin and Sarah scrambled to untie the ropes that secured it.

I looked over my shoulder.

Dr. Ames burst out the clinic door.

My legs burned, my chest ached, and I ran. I thought of my time on the treadmill. I was strong. I could do this.

Fifty feet to the boat. Forty.

Calm as ever, his boxes stacked beside him, Trent stood at the controls. He pushed the throttle, and the boat started to pull away.

"Wait!" Sarah screamed.

I tripped and almost fell, but I held the computer, stumbling forward even faster.

Thirty feet away.

Twenty. My lungs burned, and my head throbbed, but I kept running.

Dr. Ames was getting closer.

"Come on!" Quentin hurled the last line into the boat. He stood on its deck, reaching out for me.

"Catch!" I threw the computer toward him and then jumped, clinging to the railing. My body crashed into the side of the boat, and my feet splashed into the swamp, but I held on with slipping fingers until Quentin's strong arms pulled me in.

"Go!" he screamed at Trent. And the airboat took off.

I looked back. Dr. Ames was frantically untying his airboat, alone—he wasn't waiting for Dr. Gunther. I didn't hear his boat power up—ours was too loud—but I saw the propeller start to spin. "He's coming. Go faster!"

Trent frowned at the controls. "Planing at high speeds is only advisable in larger, open spaces."

Quentin shoved Trent from the controls and pushed the throttle. The fan screamed behind us. Kaylee was still in the seat where Sarah and I left her, but her eyes were open wide and terrified. No one could have slept through this.

"He's coming!" Sarah screamed from the back of the boat.

Quentin shoved the throttle forward as far as it would go, but the river turned sharply—we were back at the bend not far from Molly's camp—and the boat spun out of control.

"Hold on!" I grabbed the railing with one arm and reached for Kaylee with the other, as the airboat lurched and tipped.

The motor died.

"It's swamped!" Ben climbed over the rail and jumped into the water. It was only up to his thighs. Quentin came after him.

"Come on!" He reached up and eased Kaylee, whimpering, into the water, barefoot and still in her pajamas. "Up here!" He pointed to a mess of mangroves. "He won't be able to get the airboat up here. If he wants to follow us, he'll have to leave it and maybe . . ."

He didn't finish the sentence. Maybe what? Maybe we'd get away?

Not with Trent, who was already looking longingly back at his boxes sliding into the muck as Sarah guided him into the swamp. Not with Kaylee, who could barely walk. But I clung to her and held her up. "This way!"

We stumbled through the mud, up over the mangrove roots, but we hadn't gone more than a dozen yards when Kaylee simply went limp. Even together, Sarah and I couldn't hold her.

Kaylee whimpered. She couldn't speak, but I imagined her words, drifting up to us. *I can't go any more. I can't.* And she closed her eyes.

I eased her to the ground and stood. "Maybe we can wait it

out here," I said, but I already knew it wasn't true. Quentin had climbed into the higher branches of a mangrove. He looked out to the swamp, and his face fell. "He's off the boat. He's coming."

"Of course he's coming!" Sarah cried and sank down next to Kaylee. "All of this—this running and hiding and snakes and practically dying of thirst and these mosquitoes . . ." She slapped at one, so hard it left a red mark on her arm. "None of it matters. He'll never give up. He's never going to let go."

"What if we don't give up either? Then what?" My head throbbed, but I kept screaming. It didn't matter if Dr. Ames heard. He knew where we were, and he was coming. "What if we fight. What if—"

An osprey screamed overhead, and the words caught in my throat. Another osprey flashed in my mind, from our first day with Molly. That osprey dove for a fish and sank its talons in so deep it couldn't let go—not even when the fish was too big. Not even when holding on meant being pulled under. It died instead of letting go.

Branches cracked, and Dr. Ames's sweating face appeared below us.

"Come on!" I heaved Kaylee to her feet. "It's not far, but you have to come." I scrambled through the weeds, into the mangroves off to our right. I don't know how I knew the way—but I knew. It felt like I knew the swamp then, the way Molly knew it—and the others followed.

"Cat, watch out!" Sarah gasped. But I'd already seen the alligator—Lou. I knew she'd be there. I was counting on it.

"Up here!" I left plenty of space. We looped a wide circle

around the alligator's nest and climbed into the trees on the other side. She shifted in the dry grass and sticks, big yellow eyes following us everywhere. But she stayed on the nest.

Kaylee collapsed at the base of a mangrove, and I eased her to the ground as Dr. Ames came crashing through the trees. He stopped when he saw us. No more running. No more hiding. We stood side by side, facing him.

"Let's stop this now." His chest heaved with every breath. His clothes dripped sweat and swamp. "I don't know why you're running, or where you think you're going, but . . ."

He took a step forward and sank into the muck up to his ankles.

"We're running because we know." The words came from my mouth, but they sounded stronger than I felt. Level and even and sure.

"Oh, really? What is it you think you know?" His voice mocked me.

"We know what you did to Trent and Kaylee, what you were trying to do to us. We know everything."

He laughed and tugged his foot from the mud with a sucking slurp, then took another step in our direction.

One-Eyed Lou shifted on her nest again. The muscles in the alligator's thick body rippled, and her mouth opened slowly, in warning. Sarah's face lit up with alarm, but right away, her eyes moved back to Dr. Ames, then to me, and I knew she understood.

Dr. Ames never saw the nest. He never saw One-Eyed Lou or her babies. All he saw was the six of us, there in front of him, finally, with nowhere to run.

He never lost his focus. We were his prey, and we were cornered.

He took a flailing step forward, stumbling through the uneven mud.

And then another. "Come. With. Me." He pulled the gun from his belt and held it up so we could all see. "Now."

My heart was racing, and I could feel blood pounding in my temples, but I met his eyes. And I shook my head. "No."

His face burned so angry, so hot, I thought it might burst into flames. Sarah was right. Dr. Ames would never let go.

He lunged forward and surged through the weeds, straight at us. Straight into the alligator's nest.

Lou's tail whipped his feet out from under him and threw his body into the air.

It all happened in a heartbeat.

Dr. Ames's face twisted in surprise, the gun flew from his hand, the alligator snapped, and the shallows exploded with splashes and screams, mud and blood, and the squeaky grunts of baby alligators calling for their mother.

But she didn't answer. She thrashed and twisted, dragging the man who'd disturbed her nest deeper into the swamp water.

I had to look away, but Ben didn't. There was a battle happening in his eyes—emotions fighting for their grip on him—terror, fury, and pain.

Finally, the screams stopped, and then the splashing, and the air settled into insect buzzing and osprey cries. When I looked back at the water, the swamp had claimed whatever was left of Dr. Ames. Lou was swimming back to her nest.

I turned to Ben. The horror had drained out of his eyes, replaced by shining tears. "I believed him," he choked.

I put a hand on his arm. "I know."

We sat, trembling against the mangrove roots, until a voice cut through the humid air like a blade. "Mark! Mark!"

It was Dr. Gunther. I looked at Quentin. He held a finger to his mouth and whispered, "Careful. He could be armed, too."

But he wasn't. He rounded the bend of the river in one of the kayaks, paddling awkwardly until he came to the disabled airboat. His eyes searched the shore and finally landed on us.

"Is he . . ." He looked around. He didn't see the water at the shore, stained red.

"He's gone," I said.

Dr. Gunther stepped shakily out of the kayak.

"Wait!" I said, but it was too late. One-Eyed Lou shot across the water like a torpedo and snapped at him. Dr. Gunther fell backward over a gnarled branch, and his leg twisted at a sickening angle. His face contorted with pain. His eyes darted everywhere, terrified. But Lou was gone. There was no sign of her—only a scattering of bubbles rising in the murky water.

I held my breath—we all did—until Lou surfaced, a quiet log swimming back toward her nest, where her babies grunted for her in the grass. She climbed back onto shore facing the swamp, rearranged her prehistoric limbs, and stared out at him, cowering by the log.

"You're lucky," I said. We all were.

I turned to Quentin. "The other airboat's still okay. We can take that."

He nodded and helped me pull Kaylee up once more. She moaned softly, barely coherent. "It's okay," I said quietly. "It's going to be okay." And finally, I knew it would. At least for me. I hoped it wasn't too late for her to get to a doctor. "We're going to get you help," I promised. "A hospital where you can get better. And go home."

We eased her through the shallow water and onto the boat. She curled in a seat, shivering, and closed her eyes. Sarah climbed on board next, and then Ben.

"Trent, come on, man." Quentin sighed. Trent plucked some of his things from the swamp mud, muttering as he collected a mess of wires tangled in the weeds, and then he climbed on board.

I stood in the shallow water near the boat and looked at Dr. Gunther, struggling to stand. His leg gave out underneath him. Lou shifted on her nest.

I looked at Quentin. "Can you help me get him?"

Quentin started to climb down from the boat, but Ben grabbed his arm and whirled him around. "Are you kidding me?" Ben had said next to nothing since we left Molly's shack, but now it all came pouring out, so many days of anxiety and hurt, promises and trust betrayed. "He was going to kill us! He . . . he . . ." Ben looked as if he might leap from the boat and drown Dr. Gunther with his bare hands.

I understood. I did.

But when I looked at the old man tangled in the prison of mangrove roots, I remembered his voice back in the clinic.

Run!

He let me get away.

"He was there," I said quietly, "when I went back for the computer."

"What?" Quentin's face clouded with questions.

"When I ran to the clinic. . . ." I hoisted myself onto the edge of our swamped airboat, but I couldn't find the laptop. Had it flown into the water when we'd lost control? I spun around, searching, but it wasn't there. "Where is it? Where's the laptop?"

"Oh." Trent came over and tugged Molly's bag from behind the seat. "I put it in here to avoid potential moisture damage," he said, sliding it out of the bag. "Electronics and water don't mix."

I wanted to hug him and spin him around. The laptop was there, its video files and e-mails and research folders and memos, all preserved. The truth. I held it up. "I went back for this," I said. "Dr. Ames's laptop. And Dr. Gunther . . ." I looked at him. His eyes begged us not to leave him. "He found me in the office. But he let me go."

Ben's mouth tightened. "That doesn't matter. Not after what he did. He deserves to die here; he doesn't deserve to live. He wasn't going to let us."

No one argued with him. It was true.

Instead, Sarah moved quietly to Ben's side. She put her hand on his arm. He flinched, and his eyes were like stone. He didn't look at her, but he didn't pull away.

"You're better than that," she said quietly. "We all are."

"But I'm not," he said, and his eyes filled. "I almost got you killed. I believed *him*." He looked into the red-brown water. Wind rippled the surface. "He was the first person who actually cared about me . . . who thought I was anything at all . . ." His voice trailed off to a whisper. ". . . since my dad."

"What about your aunt and uncle?" Sarah said quietly.

Ben shook his head. "My aunt's okay. But my uncle . . ." He shrugged. "He never wanted kids." He closed his eyes, squeezed them tight, but a tear spilled out. He shrugged and looked back at the water. There was nothing left where Dr. Ames had been. "I wanted to believe him so much."

Sarah let her hand drop to Ben's and squeezed. "It's okay," she said. "It's okay."

"No, it's not." Ben glared at Dr. Gunther, leaning back weakly in the water. Then he looked at us, eyes shining, wet. "I knew. And I lied to you."

I didn't know what to say.

Sarah shifted her weight. "If it makes you feel any better, I lied, too."

"About what?" I asked.

"I didn't get checked into the boards at hockey. I tripped over my skate lace while I was going to get nachos and knocked my head on the concrete steps of the bleachers."

Quentin paused, then bit his lip. "Yeah . . . well . . . my football injury . . . didn't actually happen while playing school football. I kind of fell over my dog."

"Your *dog* took you out?" Ben almost smiled.

"I *was* playing football," Quentin said quickly, "in the park with my little brother. But yeah. I tripped over Baxter."

Sarah laughed. "Well, I feel better now." She reached out for Ben's hand. Ben hesitated, then took it and held on, tears in his eyes. "What about you, Cat? Going to come clean on the real story of your concussion?"

"Seriously," I said, "if I were going to lie about what happened to me, don't you think I'd come up with something less dorky than falling out of a tree stand watching birds?"

This time, Ben laughed.

"Shall I start this up?" Trent asked from the front of the working airboat. "When we get back to town, I'd like to stop somewhere and purchase dry batteries."

"You got it, man. Give me one minute." Quentin turned back to Ben. "We need to take Dr. Gunther with us."

Ben didn't answer.

It was easy to understand why Ben would want to leave him, after everything we'd been through. But it felt wrong. And I was through letting Dr. Ames—or anybody—decide what kind of person I was going to be.

I looked at Ben. Then at Dr. Gunther. "If we leave him," I said quietly, "he's going to die. I can't do that."

Finally, Ben nodded. He didn't help us as we lifted Dr. Gunther from the water and eased him onto the boat. But he didn't try to stop us either.

I climbed onto the boat and nodded at Trent. "Ready."

A lone osprey soared overhead. It followed us all the way past the island with the poachers' hut, past Molly's camp. "Thank you," I whispered. She had kept her promise to us, after all. We were going home.

The osprey didn't leave us. It followed us out of the mangrove tunnels. It dipped and rose again as we pulled up to the dock at

Camilla's Grille, then hovered for a moment, as if it were making sure we'd be okay.

And we are, I thought, climbing off the boat. *We made it. We're going to be okay.*

I looked up, wiped away a tear, and watched the osprey, finally, fly away.

35

WHEN WE PULLED UP TO the dock at Camilla's Grille—six wet, muddy kids and an old man, lying half-conscious on the airboat's deck—the waitress almost dropped her tray of ketchup. It was Kelly, the one who had waited on Mom and me, and she came rushing right out.

It had been hard to explain to the others why I figured we could trust somebody I only met once, when she brought me a quesadilla. "She's a mom," I'd told them. "She'll help us. If that investigative reporter's not around, she'll help us find him."

But she didn't need to.

Brady Kenyon was there at the bar, in that same seat, drinking coffee with his notebook beside him.

"What in the devil happened to you kids?" he asked, already reaching for a pen.

"We have a news story for you," I told him.

Kelly called for an ambulance, then brought us water and ibuprofen. Quentin and Ben took Kaylee to rest at a picnic table while they waited, and Sarah walked with Trent to check out the basket-ball court behind the restaurant. I watched Sarah make a few layups, then toss the ball to Trent, who studied it for a minute and then, with perfect form, sank a basket from the far end of the court. Sarah cheered, but Trent looked genuinely surprised when it went in. Maybe our muscles hold on to memories better than our minds.

"You ready?" Brady Kenyon said, flipping to a clean page in his reporter's notebook.

And I told him our story.

I started at the beginning, my lunch with Mom that felt like it happened in some other lifetime.

I told him everything . . . right up to when we pulled up at the dock.

Kelly put a hand on my shoulder as she set another glass of water in front of me. "I tried calling your parents, but your aunt said they were already on the plane, sweetie, halfway here. They're on their way. All the families are."

I remembered what Dr. Gunther told them, and my heart twisted. "Do they know I'm okay?"

"They will very soon," she promised.

My eyes welled up. I hadn't really let myself cry this week, but now, knowing Mom and Dad were coming, I felt like I could almost let go. But not quite.

I blinked fast, took a drink of water, and startled when I heard an ambulance pull into the gravel driveway. It sounded too much like the smugglers' truck at the dock. I took a deep breath. This whole awful mess was beginning to feel real, like it hadn't been some bad dream.

A second ambulance came. A door slammed, and my heart leaped into my throat again. Would the rest of my life be like this? Full of plain old regular noises that were terrifying because they brought me back to the swamp?

"Don't worry." Brady Kenyon watched with me as EMTs gently eased Kaylee onto a stretcher and lifted her into the first ambulance. "They're going to take great care of her. Pete and Jim'll be with her the whole time, too."

Pete and Jim were two of the four U.S. Fish and Wildlife agents Brady Kenyon had called. He promised they were all friends of his who had already been investigating Dr. Gunther for importing illegal butterflies. Pete and Jim stood by the ambulance, along with Sarah and Quentin, then climbed in next to Kaylee before it pulled away.

Quentin and Sarah waved and wiped away tears, then walked over to join Trent at a nearby picnic table. Kelly had given him the restaurant's broken toaster to take apart.

The second ambulance pulled forward, and medics loaded Dr. Gunther into the back.

"What's going to happen to him?" I asked.

"They'll set his broken leg. Then he'll have a lot of questions to answer."

Dr. Gunther's eyes fell on me before the ambulance door slammed shut. They were sad and full of sorry. But it wasn't enough. It could never be enough.

"I don't understand how he could . . . how anybody . . ." I stopped. There weren't words for what they'd done.

Brady Kenyon leaned back in his chair and crossed his arms.

I thought he was watching the ambulance, but his eyes stared at the same spot even after it pulled away. Finally, he shook his head. "I don't know," he said, and tapped the laptop computer that rested on our table, between my water and my untouched turkey sandwich, "but from the few videos you've already shown me, it sounds like Dr. Ames and Senator Wiley had something on Gunther."

"Like he was in trouble?" I remembered the way Dr. Gunther cowered in the video and understood he'd been afraid of Dr. Ames long before I was. "He was sick, too," I suddenly remembered. "Dr. Ames said Dr. Gunther was going to die if he couldn't continue his research."

"That would explain why Gunther cooperated." Kenyon's eyes scanned the long list of video files—hours of clinic activity Dr. Ames had never expected anyone outside of the project to see.

"Did you have any idea?" I asked. "That time you visited the clinic? Did you have any idea what was going on?"

He shook his head. "No. I was working on an investigative piece about wildlife poaching. Got a tip about Gunther's endangered bird-wing," he said.

I remembered the butterflies—brilliant and delicate, frozen forever in time on Dr. Gunther's wall. If he hadn't been obsessed with collecting them, would Dr. Ames have gotten away with everything? I shivered, even though the sun had crept around the umbrella that stuck up from our table.

"So, let me ask you one more question. I had talked with Sawgrass Molly last week, looking for leads on the poaching story. How did you know to find me here? Had she mentioned that to you?"

"No. But I found this in her bag." I pulled the waterlogged business card from my pocket and handed it to him. "You gave it to her?"

He nodded. "She was a great source out there. Told her to call me anytime she thought somebody was up to no good out in the islands."

"But she didn't tell you about us?"

He shook his head.

Maybe she meant to. Maybe Brady Kenyon was the person she was going to call to help us, but she never had the chance. "She's . . . we had to leave her body there, at the shack. Will you . . ."

He nodded. "I'll make sure she's taken care of. She loved that swamp."

My eyes watered, remembering Molly at the helm of her boat, pointing out the crab traps and alligators.

"So, you found my card with her things?" His voice brought me back from the swamp.

I nodded. "And I remembered your name."

He tipped his head. "Remembered my name from where? I've never met you before."

"You were here the day I had lunch with my mom, before . . ." Before everything. I pointed to the bar. "You were sitting there, and Kelly said, 'Hey, Brady,' and she asked if you wanted your usual, so I knew you came here a lot."

"What if I hadn't been here?"

"I knew you might not be, but I figured she would." I pointed to Kelly, taking orders a couple tables over. "And I knew . . ." I hesitated. It sounded dumb. I didn't know Kelly, hadn't said a word to her except to order the quesadilla I never ate. But it was true. "I knew she'd help us. She's a mom."

Tires crunched on the driveway. I jumped in my seat, then sighed. It was another U.S. Fish and Wildlife van, and when it pulled to a stop next to the picnic table, my parents flew out the door.

They didn't see me right away. Mom looked at Quentin and Ben, at Trent with his toaster pieces, at Sarah, then turned. When she saw me, her face melted into a million different emotions—joy and relief and remorse and pain. But mostly love.

"Mom!" I jumped up and ran into the biggest, longest, strangler-fig hug of my life. I buried my face in her damp T-shirt and breathed her in. Dad wrapped his arms around both of us, and Mom started shaking.

She was crying. Everything was okay.

Finally, I let all the pieces I'd been holding together come apart, and I cried with her, with Dad, all wrapped up in their arms.

Tires crunching on gravel startled me again, and I pulled back from Mom and Dad to look. A third Fish and Wildlife van had arrived with the other parents. They must have all booked flights when Dr. Gunther called with his awful lies. Back home, Mom freaked out if I even came back from a bike ride late; I couldn't imagine what those hours had been like for her and Dad, believing I was gone.

But now we were here . . . together.

Sarah sat on the picnic table bench, leaning against her mom, a woman with Sarah's same dark-brown hair and green eyes. She was clinging to Sarah every bit as tightly as Mom was hugging me.

Quentin was invisible, buried in a double hug with his mom and dad.

Ben sat between his aunt and uncle. His aunt gushed over him, wiping away tears. His uncle held his face in his hands, sobbing.

Kelly was talking quietly to Trent, who was half listening while he tightened a screw on the toaster. His foster parents had gotten the news that he was alive, but that he'd been part of an unsanctioned experiment, and that he was . . . different from the boy they'd said good-bye to six weeks ago.

I wondered if it was true that the genetic engineering could be reversed. I wanted to meet the real Trent someday—the old Trent who made Sarah laugh. I hoped he was still alive in there, somewhere.

And Kaylee—were her parents at the hospital already? A lump grew in my throat, and I prayed as hard as I could that it wasn't too late for her parents to get their daughter back, too.

Mom pulled me closer. "Cat. Cat. Thank God. I can't wait to get you home."

I wanted to go home more than anything. But not quite yet.

"Hey, Mom . . . Dad . . . you need to meet some people." I introduced them to Quentin and Sarah and Ben and Trent, and we had a whole new round of hugging and tears, until finally, the Fish and Wildlife guys waiting in the van climbed out.

"Let's get you to the hospital so doctors can check you over; it was quite an ordeal you went through. And I know you must be exhausted, but after that, we need you all to come by head-quarters. We have some federal agents waiting there to take your statements. And we'll keep a record of everything, too."

Quentin and Ben climbed into the first van with Quentin's parents and Ben's aunt and uncle. Kelly went with Trent; his foster parents wouldn't arrive in Miami until later, so she sat next to him in the van, calmly handing him toaster parts and tools as if being surrogate mother and assistant to a teen science prodigy were something she did every day.

Sarah climbed into the other van with her mom and waved for me and my parents to come, too. As I was about to get in, Brady Kenyon rushed over from his table with Dr. Ames's laptop closed and tucked under his arm. "I need to turn this over for evidence, okay?" He nodded toward the Fish and Wildlife guys. "They'll pass it along to the federal agents."

I hesitated. "You can't just give it to them. What if—"

"Relax." He waved a small storage drive. "It's all right here. Every single file. I put it all on my laptop and made three more copies, too. One is on its way to the newspaper in Miami with a friend of mine. I'm putting one in a safe-deposit box. Another one's going home with Kelly. And this one's for you." He held the tiny black storage drive out to me.

"Thanks." It was warm in my hand. I started to put it in my pocket but hesitated. Part of me wanted to get as far away from this story as I could. Bury it somewhere and never think about it again. But I knew I had to keep it, so I gave it to my mom, and she put it in her purse.

I looked back at the van. "So, these guys are okay?" He'd

promised we could trust the Fish and Wildlife officers, and I wanted to.

"They're honest as the day is long," he said. "I'm not going to lie to you, though. With Senator Wiley involved, it's hard to say how deep this goes. But as long as we have this"—he pulled another storage drive from his pocket—"nobody can lie about what happened out there. Your story's not going to get lost."

"When is it going to be in the newspaper?" Mom asked him.

"I'm guessing we've only scratched the surface, even with our long conversation today, so I'm going to do a lot more digging, and I'm sure we'll run more than one story. But the first one?" He looked at his watch. "If I get moving, it'll break tomorrow morning." His eyes were alive with excitement or determination or . . . whatever it was, I trusted him. He would tell the truth about the miracle clinic in the swamp. And that was enough to make sure what happened to us could never happen to anyone else.

"It's an incredible story, Cat. What you guys went through . . . you're an amazing bunch of kids."

"Thanks." The van was running. Mom and Dad were waiting. And I was ready to go home. "You have everything you need for the article?" I asked.

"Between these videos and the story you told me?" He nodded. "Enough for a whole book."

36

MIAMI HERALD
Tuesday, May 23

US SENATOR FACES SECRET SCIENCE CONSPIRACY CHARGES

MIAMI . . . US Senator R. J. Wiley was taken into custody late last night in connection with a plot to perform illegal experiments on six youths at what was once regarded as the nation's premiere head-injury clinic, the International Center for Advanced Neurology, known as I-CAN, located at a former military property in the Everglades.

Wiley, who served as chairman of the Senate Armed Services Committee, resigned from both his committee post and his Senate seat early this morning. He is accused of conspiracy and kidnapping, and officials say more charges may follow.

The conspiracy involved a plan to use reconstructed DNA

WAKE UP MISSING

from history's most notable scientists and inventors, combined with implanted computer microchips, to create modern-day prodigies for use in weapons research. The six subjects, whose names are being withheld to protect their privacy, had been entrusted to the care of the renowned clinic after they were diagnosed with severe post-concussion syndrome. They managed to escape from their captors after a plot to move them to a new location was foiled by a routine Drug Enforcement Agency roadblock.

All six patients have now been reunited with their parents and guardians. Four sustained no major injuries or illnesses. However, doctors at Everglades City Hospital say one patient has been diagnosed with a brain tumor they believe may be linked to her time at I-CAN, and a second patient who had undergone experiments seems to have had adverse reactions as well. Doctors are not releasing further details at the request of the patients' families.

Police interviews with the four healthy patients led them to a gruesome discovery in the swamp. The body of Molly Louise Turner, "Sawgrass Molly," as she was known to locals, was discovered in an abandoned plume hunters' camp not far from the clinic. Investigators say she died of a gunshot wound to the head. Records show that the clinic occasionally employed Turner to bring patients to the facility via airboat, and police are investigating whether or not her death may be connected to the clinic.

But evidence may be hard to come by. The I-CAN compound itself burned last night. Officials aren't sure if the blaze was arson or if the buildings were consumed by the wildfires that have ravaged South Florida in the past five weeks of drought and lightning.

Investigators will spend this week sifting through the remains of the facility for evidence, but they believe all of the clinic's papers and equipment were destroyed.

However, one of the young patients escaped with a facility-owned laptop computer, and digital security-camera records recovered from its hard drive show multiple video recordings of two doctors discussing the project. Clearly audible conversations make it apparent that they were aware of one patient's rapidly declining health and chose not to notify her family in order to keep the project secret. Additional files recovered from the computer suggest that the clinic operators used retroviruses, a common gene-therapy technique, to introduce genetic material from long-dead scientists into the damaged brain tissue of concussion patients. The computer also contained numerous folders with research information on such notable scientists as Thomas Edison, Marie Curie, Albert Einstein, and Robert Oppenheimer.

Officials are investigating leads that suggest the genetic-engineering program may have been part of a larger government project to create a new super-weapon for use against Al-Jihada and other international terrorist groups. However, Senator Thomas Huggler, Wiley's colleague on the Armed Services Committee, denies any knowledge of the program.

"We are shocked and horrified at this news," Huggler said in a phone interview from his residence in Houston. "If investigators find that Senator Wiley was indeed part of such a conspiracy, I can assure you that it was on his own, without the knowledge of this committee."

US Attorney General Russell McNair says his office is

conducting a full investigation, and there will likely be Congres-
sional hearings as well.

In addition to Senator Wiley, the clinic's two staff physicians,
Dr. Rudolph Gunther and Dr. Mark Ames, also face charges. Gun-
ther, who has recently been the target of an unrelated U.S. Fish and
Wildlife investigation into illegal trafficking of endangered butter-
flies, is in the Everglades City hospital recovering from a broken
leg and is cooperating with investigators. Ames, who is the nephew
of Senator R. J. Wiley, is missing after reportedly being attacked by
an alligator in the swamp. He is believed to be dead, but officials
have yet to recover his remains.

I set the newspaper aside.

"Well?" Mom looks at me across the table.

"He pretty much included everything. Now what?"

"Now . . ." She eyes the paper, then looks over at Dad. "Now
they'll do their investigation and try to find out who knew what . . .
whether it was Senator Wiley acting on his own, or if the whole
thing runs deeper than that."

"Do you think they'll find out the truth?"

Shades of maybe pass over their faces like colors on the mood
ring Aunt Beth bought me at the fair once. They want to promise
me yes, of course they'll learn the truth. But they don't lie.

"They'll try," Dad says.

"I hope so," Mom says. "But no matter what, you're safe
now." She stretches past her coffee and my orange juice to brush
my hair behind my ear, then comes over and wraps her arms
around me.

All morning since we checked out of the inn and settled in for breakfast before our flight home, she's been reaching over to touch me. First my hand, then my cheek, then a palm under my chin, as if she can't quite be sure it's me.

But it is.

The same old Cat. Mostly.

Fiddler crabs scuttle between the weathered deck planks under our table, and the rising red-orange sun glitters on the rippling water.

Kelly comes out of the kitchen, tying her apron behind her. "So, what'll it be this morning?"

"Eggs and home fries with toast, please," Dad says.

"I'll have two poached eggs and a grapefruit, please," Mom says.

"Chocolate chip pancakes for me. Thanks." I hand Kelly the menu. "Thanks for everything."

"Can't imagine what you folks went through. If this had happened to my boys . . ." She shakes her head, tears welling in her eyes, and gives me a quick hug before she leaves for the kitchen with her order pad.

Somewhere, from over the trees, an osprey calls, and I smile. But my eyes fill up with tears.

"Sweetie, are you all right? Does your head hurt?" Mom reaches for my hand.

"No, it feels okay. That medicine's working." The doctors at Everglades City Hospital gave us the same kind of medicine Dr. Ames had at the clinic, and even though that creeped me out, it worked. Most of what they'd done at I-CAN, leading up to Phase

Three, was actually good for us—the oxygen and light therapy and exercise—so I'll keep getting those treatments once I get home. They've already helped so much.

But none of it can erase what happened, and that's why I can't stop crying.

"What is it?" Dad leans forward and squints at me, but there's nothing he can see. No scratch or bee sting or bruise. Some hurts are invisible on the outside.

Mom rummages in her backpack and pulls out a linty tissue. "Thanks. It's just . . . hard."

"I bet." Mom takes a deep breath, holds it, and sighs. "I wish there were more we could do."

"Yeah." But there isn't. I told Mom and Dad everything that happened in the swamp. Everything I could. But there's so much I can't explain.

In some ways, I'm the same Cat—same brown eyes, same freckles, same sweet tooth, even at breakfast—but in other ways, I know I'll never be the same again. And it's not just the experiments or the medicine at the clinic that changed me.

I don't know if I'll ever look at a doctor the same way, or read a news story without wondering which parts of it are really true. I do know I'll never turn away from someone who needs a friend. I've promised myself that.

"I'm all right," I say. "It's a lot to think about, is all."

Mom reaches over and tucks my hair again, even though it's barely had time to come untucked.

"I'm okay. Really."

But I wish I had a crystal ball to tell me if Kaylee will be okay, if Trent will ever get his old personality and memories back. But I don't. So I can only wait for news.

About Sarah and Quentin and Ben, too.

I hope lots of things for them . . . that Quentin will get great report cards and a scholarship someday, one to make his grandma proud.

That Sarah will get to play hockey again, that she'll win every game and somehow get better at math and meet a boy she likes as much as she liked Trent.

I hope things get better for Ben so he can ride horses again, and laugh. I hope one day he understands, really knows in his heart, that he matters.

I hope their lives will be good ones.

And I have hopes for me, too. As soon as I get home, back to my clay, I'm going to start a new osprey sculpture.

I want to run cross-country next year.

I want to join art club with Amberlee.

And I hope things work out with Lucy, too. She called while I was away, Mom said, and she wants to come over when I get home. Maybe that means we'll be friends again, but I won't give up who I am to make it happen.

That's one way I'm a little different.

But I'm still me.

It's more than I can explain to Mom and Dad. So I tell them again, as Kelly sets down the pancakes and I reach for my fork, "I'm okay."

They nod like it makes sense. But they weren't there with me, at the clinic and all through the swamp. So there's no way they can understand the mix of flying joy and squeezing awful sadness that caught my heart when I heard that osprey cry.

But it's a part of me now—like Molly, and Quentin, Sarah, Ben, and Trent and Kaylee, like One-Eyed Lou and the water that fell from the sky into the air plants to wait for us when we needed it most. It's all a part of me now, sure as my DNA.

If you weren't there, if you didn't almost lose everything— lose *yourself*—you can't understand what it's like to wake up missing— and then, like a gift, get yourself back.

AUTHOR'S NOTE

Both *Wake Up Missing* and my previous novel *Eye of the Storm* (2012) are science thrillers. The spark for *Eye of the Storm* was a combination of things—a news piece about the possible impacts that climate change could have on weather and an article about a physicist who believed that blasting thunderstorms with microwave beams might stop tornadoes from forming. Those news features made me wonder . . . What if the weather got worse? And what if some of us learned how to control it? Those "what if" questions get my mind spinning, and sometimes, it all comes out in a book.

Wake Up Missing began that way, too. I'd seen a news report on the epidemic of concussions among high school athletes in the United States and the effects that post-concussion syndrome could have on kids' sports careers, academic lives, friendships, and very selves. I've always been interested in genetics—what makes a person *that* particular person—and those two ideas combined to create Cat's story.

While *Wake Up Missing* is a work of fiction, you'll find lots of real science within the story. Some of the concussion treatments in the book are being used in real hospitals and clinics or being studied as possible treatments. A 2009 study reported that some members of the US military who'd suffered traumatic brain injuries or suffered from post-concussion syndrome improved after receiving hyperbaric oxygen treatments—something that had been used to treat sick divers in the past. Learn more at http://www.ncbi.nlm.nih.gov/pmc/articles/PMC2740054/. The study has gotten some attention, and this treatment is now being used more often for athletes with concussions.

There's also early research to suggest that the kind of LED light therapy used at I-CAN could help real-world patients with concussions. The National Center for Biotechnology Information described the procedure and findings in two case studies: http://www.ncbi.nlm.nih.gov/pmc/articles/PMC3104287/.

What about Cat's time on the treadmill? The State University of New York at Buffalo used a similar program of exercise therapy for athletes recovering from concussions, and so far, it seems to be helping. The exercise-therapy program runs on the same theory Dr. Ames described in *Wake Up Missing*—that exercise may help to "reset" the regulatory system responsible for regulating blood flow to the brain, which can be affected by concussions. You can read more about the research here: http://www.buffalo.edu/news/10848. The UB Concussion Clinic also has a great website with information about concussions and links to video and other media coverage of their work: http://concussion.buffalo.edu/.

While I haven't come across any research on gene therapy as a treatment for concussions, it is being studied as a possible treatment for a number of illnesses and conditions including inherited blindness, some cancers, and Parkinson's disease, which the National Institute of Health says affects an estimated half million real Americans, in addition to the fictional Dr. Gunther.

You may want to check out the links below to learn more about the science and history behind *Wake Up Missing*:

As Quentin tells Cat, the idea of getting together a team of brilliant minds to solve a problem isn't a new one. You can read more about the Manhattan Project during World War II here: http://www.britannica.com/EBchecked/topic/362098/Manhattan -Project.

The term "a new Manhattan Project" is sometimes used to describe this sort of scientific team effort. Here's a National Public Radio (NPR) story on a more current project, focused on the issues of childhood obesity and nutrition: http://www.npr.org /blogs/thesalt/2012/09/19/161444045/billionaires-fund-a-manhat tan-project-for-nutrition-and-obesity.

Would a government ever really do experiments on its citizens without providing them with information and getting consent? History has a precedent for this, too. The United States Holocaust Memorial Museum tells the story of Nazi medical experiments on thousands of concentration camp prisoners during World War II: http://www.ushmm.org/wlc/en/article.php?ModuleId=10005168.

And in the 1930s, the U.S. Public Health Service and the Tuskegee Institute conducted a study on almost four hundred poor black men to try to learn how the disease syphilis affects people.

The researchers told the men they were getting treatment for "bad blood" (a vague phrase used to describe any number of ailments at that time), but they were never told they had syphilis or treated for it. In fact, treatment was withheld from the men, even after it became available, so researchers could learn more about how the disease spreads. NPR did a story called "Remembering Tuskegee" on the anniversary of the day this news broke: http://www.npr .org/programs/morning/features/2002/jul/tuskegee/.

While the kind of genetic engineering that happens in *Wake Up Missing* isn't technically possible right now, it's interesting to think about where genetic engineering will go next. Already, there are concerns about gene doping in future Olympics. This feature in *U.S. News* asks the question, could athletes modify their genetic makeup to improve their chances of winning gold?: http:// health.usnews.com/health-news/news/articles/2012/07/26/could -gene-doping-be-part-of-future-olympics.

And what else might be on the horizon? A Nature.com feature explores the possibility of both gene doping and "designer babies":

http://www.nature.com/scitable/topicpage/genetic-inequality -human-genetic-engineering-768.

"Will our kids be a different species?" Juan Enriquez, the founder of the Life Sciences Project at Harvard Business School, gave this TED talk about bioengineering and how it just might lead us to evolve. His ideas on both cloning and "downloading memories" served as inspiration for Trent's story. Find the video at http://www.ted.com/talks/juan_enriquez_will_our_kids_be_a_ different_species.html.

How quickly will this high-tech field move in the years to come? Certainly, ethics will play a major role. The United States and United Nations have already created bioethics groups to study these issues and recommend policies to regulate them, so we probably won't see the kinds of projects that happen in this book anytime soon. But the research and advances in technology will likely keep us asking just what it means to be a person, and how far is too far when it comes to building a better human.

ACKNOWLEDGMENTS

Writing *Wake Up Missing* was a process almost as challenging and confusing as Cat's journey to rediscover herself, and I am so very grateful to the people who offered help along the way. The naturalist guides with Everglades Adventure and Ivey House in Everglades City were patient, kind, and informative when I asked more than my share of questions on several guided kayak trips into the swamp, and Tod Dahike at Tour the Glades kindly provided me with information about hiking in the Fakahatchee Strand. Any errors in the book are mine alone.

My critique partners, Loree Griffin Burns, Eric Luper, and Liza Martz, read the earliest draft of this book and offered valuable feedback on my characters and plot twists. Writer friend Linda Urban offered more thoughts, title inspiration, and a couple of long conversations that helped missing pieces settle into place later on. Readers and friends Bethany and Jenna Ward also offered great feedback and encouragement on an early draft.

Thanks to my agent, Jennifer Laughran of the Andrea Brown

Literary Agency, for being the best and smartest advocate a writer could ever want, and to my editor, Mary Kate Castellani, who is kind, smart, and funny, and always knows the right questions to ask to make me a better writer.

Thanks to Sandra Smith, Amanda Hong, Sammy Yuen Jr., Ilana Worrell, Emily Easton, Beth Eller, Linette Kim, Katy Hershberger, and the rest of the Walker/Bloomsbury team for bringing my books into the world.

I'm grateful to my mom and dad, Tom and Gail Schirmer, who have been encouraging me and reading my stories for more than thirty years now. And finally, to my family—Tom, Jake, and Ella— you are the best. Thanks for your support, laughter, and love, always.